Lincoln Financial Foundation

Thanksgiving Proclamation

Lincoln Financial Foundation

Thanksgiving Proclamation

ISBN/EAN: 9783741104978

Manufactured in Europe, USA, Canada, Australia, Japa

Cover: Foto ©Andreas Hilbeck / pixelio.de

Manufactured and distributed by brebook publishing software
(www.brebook.com)

Lincoln Financial Foundation

Thanksgiving Proclamation

Thanksgiving Proclamation

Proclamations

Excerpts from newspapers and other sources

From the files of the

Lincoln Financial Foundation Collection

NATIONAL THANKSGIVING.

PROCLAMATION BY HORATIO SEYMOUR, GOVERNOR OF THE STATE OF NEW YORK.

Whereas, the President of the United States has set apart Thursday, the 6th day of August, to be observed as a day of national thanksgiving and praise for the great victories recently gained by our armies and navies; I, Horatio Seymour, Governor of New York, do hereby request the people of this State to observe that day in the manner and for the purpose recommended by the Chief Magistrate of this Union.

Humbly acknowledging our dependence upon Almighty God, let us assemble in our respective places of public worship, and with heartfelt gratitude thank Him for our national successes. Let us pour forth fervent prayers for His blessings upon those who have periled their lives in desperate conflicts to uphold the constitution of our country and to maintain that Union of these States which is essential to the peace and happiness of our people. In the midst our rejoicing, let us remember those whose homes have been made desolate by the ravages of war. Let us offer up our petitions that our people may be animated by virtue, intelligence and patriotism, and that our rulers may be endowed with wisdom to put down rebellion, to uphold the liberties and rights of our people, and to restore the blessings of peace, order and prosperity to our afflicted country.

In witness whereof I have hereunto set my name and affixed the privy seal of the State, at the city of Albany, this 3d day of August, in the year of our Lord 1863,

HORATIO SEYMOUR.

By the Governor:
DANIEL F. TYLER, Private Secretary.

THANKSGIVING.

Proclamation by the President.

WASHINGTON, Oct. 21.—The following proclamation was promulgated this afternoon:

By the President of the United States of America.

A PROCLAMATION.

It has pleased Almighty God to prolong our national life another year, defending us with His guardian care against unfriendly designs from abroad, and vouchsafing us in His mercy many and signal victories over the enemy who is of our household. It has also pleased our Heavenly Father to favor as well our citizens in their homes as our soldiers in their camps and our sailors on the rivers and seas, with unusual health.

He has largely augmented our free population by emancipation and by immigration, while He has opened to us new resources of wealth, and has crowned the labor of our workingmen in every department of industry with abundant reward.

Moreover, He has been pleased to animate and inspire our minds and hearts with fortitude, courage and resolution sufficient for the great trial of civil war into which we have been brought by our adherence as a nation to the cause of freedom and humanity, and to afford to us reasonable hopes of an ultimate and happy deliverance from all our dangers and afflictions.

Now therefore, I, Abraham Lincoln, President of the United States, do hereby appoint and set apart the last Thursday in November next, as a day which I desire to be observed by all my fellow-citizens, wherever they may then be, as a day of thanksgiving and praise to Almighty God, the beneficent Creator and Ruler of the Universe.

And I do further recommend to my fellow-citizens aforesaid, that on that occasion they do reverently humble themselves in the dust, and from thence offer up penitent and fervent prayers and supplications to the Great Disposer of events for a return of the inestimable blessings of Peace, Union and Harmony throughout the land which it has pleased Him to assign as a dwelling place for ourselves, and for our posterity throughout all generations.

In testimony whereof I have hereunto set my hand, and caused the seal of the United States to be affixed.

Done at the city of Washington this 20th day of October, in the year of our Lord one thousand eight hundred and sixty-four, and of the independence of the United States the eighty-ninth.

ABRAHAM LINCOLN.

By the President:

WILLIAM H. SEWARD,
Secretary of State.

FROM WASHINGTON.

Proclamation by President Lincoln.

A Day of Thanksgiving Appointed for the Last Thursday in November.

WASHINGTON, October 21.

The following proclamation was promulgated this afternoon :—

By the President of the United States of America :

A PROCLAMATION.

It has pleased Almighty God to prolong our national life another year, defending us with His guardian care against unfriendly designs from abroad, and vouchsafing to us in His mercy many and signal victories over the enemy who is of our own household. It has also pleased our Heavenly Father to favor as well our citizens in their homes as our soldiers in their camps and our sailors on the rivers and seas with unusual health. He has largely augmented our free population by emancipation and by immigration, while He has opened to us new sources of wealth, and has crowned the labor of our working men in every department of industry with abundant reward. Moreover he has been pleased to animate and inspire our minds and hearts with fortitude, courage and resolution sufficient for the great trial of civil war, into which we have been brought by our adherence, as a nation, to the cause of freedom and humanity, and to afford to us reasonable hopes of an ultimate and happy deliverance from all our dangers and afflictions.

Now, therefore, I, Abraham Lincoln, President of the United States, do hereby appoint and set apart the last Thursday in November next as a day which I desire to to be observed by all my fellow citizens whereover they may then be, as a day of thanksgiving and prayer to Almighty God, the beneficent Creator and Ruler of the universe, and I do further recommend to my fellow-citizens aforesaid, that on that occasion they do reverently humble themselves in the dust, and from thence offer up penitent and fervent prayers and supplications to the Great Disposer of events for a return of the inestimable blessings of peace, union, and harmony throughout the land which it has pleased Him to assign as a dwelling-place for ourselves and our posterity throughout all generations.

In testimony whereof I have hereunto set my hand and caused the seal of the United States to be affixed. Done at the City of Washington, this 20th day of October, in the year of Our Lord 1864, and of the independence of the United States the eighty-ninth.

ABRAHAM LINCOLN.

By the President,

WM. H. SEWARD, Secretary of State.

AULD LANG SYNE.

The Thanksgiving Celebrations of Former Years.

IN WAR-TIME AND LATER.

Some Famous Proclamations —Old-Time Preachers, and Sermons Minus Sensationalism — Brief Recollections of Stage Favorites.

Woe unto the turkey gobbler for his days are numbered and are very few. The annual attack on the barnyard favorite will be held, according to the good old custom, on Thursday, November 28, rain, snow, or shine. It will take about 50,000 good, fat, tender, young and juicy gobblers to make everyone in Buffalo feel comfortable and happy this Thanksgiving Day. It has been a year of abundant crops, "good times" are rapidly returning, and good cheer should prevail on this National festival day. The observance of a special day for prayer, praise, and thanksgiving, originated in New England, and was first recognized as a National holiday by President Lincoln in 1862, during the darkest days of the Civil War. A brief review of some of the most important observances of Thanksgiving Day in Buffalo since that time may prove of interest to old and young alike.

A War Governor's Paper.

On October 1, 1862, Governor E. D. Morgan, at Albany, issued a proclamation requesting the people of this State to observe Thursday, November 27, "as a day of Praise, Thanksgiving, and Prayer to Almighty God." It was a wise, patriotic, aye, prophetic document, and is here republished in part:

"From the depths of National affliction we come, with stricken hearts and chastened spirits, to own our dependence upon the Most High, and to render, with grateful sense, our thanksgiving for His mercies, countless in number and infinite in extent. A year fraught with the heaviest sorrows has yet, in the merciful plan of Providence been distinguished by the most conspicuous blessings. Although it is numbered among the dark periods of history, and its sorrowful records are graven on many hearthstones, yet the precious blood shed in the cause of our country will hallow and strengthen our love and our reverence for it and its institutions, while the bitter sorrows of the year will discipline us into humility. Whatever was passionate in the early period of the War has given way to a deep and subdued conviction of duty in defending the integrity of the Union. Reflection has made clear our obligations, and the issues of the momentous struggle are sent themselves in more definite form. Our National aims have been elevated, and our sacrifices have made us less selfish; our Government and institutions placed in jeopardy have brought us to a more just appreciation of their value. Looking beyond the wicked leaders, who have precipitated this terrible calamity of civil war upon us, we see that the people in arms against the Government possess the higher qualities of our national character; and though their minds have been perverted by passion and prejudice, yet on many occasions their prowess and devotion to their cause has been such as to win our respect. We are permitted to see that the war is developing the manhood of the Nation; and when peace shall return, we have faith that the American Republic will be more powerful, the Government more permanent, the elements of society more perfectly blended, and the people more firmly united than ever.

"We have other causes for gratitude. Disease has been averted at home; the unanimated armies have been kept protected from pestilences which it was feared would follow them in distant latitudes. Earth's best fruits have been lavishly bestowed, the arts have prospered, the employments of peace have been rewarded, and the good order of society has been fully maintained. Reverses to our arms have been followed by successes on land and sea which specially call for thanksgiving, and justify the most sanguine expectations as to the final result of the contest."

The day in 1862 was "damp and chilly," 'tis recorded, "and not well calculated to excite a love for outside demonstrations." Among the preachers that day were Dr. Stover, Methodist; Dr. Chester and Barnham, Presbyterian; Dr. Hosmer, Unitarian. At St. Paul's, Dr. Pitkin of Albany preached; at St. Joseph's, Bishop Timon; at the old Washington Street Baptist Church, Dr. Marshall of the Cedar Street Church officiated.

That patriotic scribe, Almon M. Clapp was Postmaster of Buffalo, then and patriotically closed the Postoffice at 12:30 p. m. "for the balance of the day." In the line of amusements, the Buffalonians of '61 had Carlotta Patti at American Hall, Miss Nellie Hindley, "the celebrated vocalist and danseuse," at Curr's Melodeon and W. H. Leak as Luke in "The Willow Copse" at the Metropolitan Theater. John H. Meech, manager. Company F, 7th Regiment, Capt. Hugh Mion, gave a ball at American Hall on Thanksgiving Eve; at Kremlin Hall there was a masquerade and at "Flock's Hall on Batavia Street" the Seymour and Ganson Club of the 6th Ward gave a dance. A beautiful prayer written for the occasion by Bishop Delancey, then head of the Episcopal diocese of Buffalo, was recited in all of the Episcopal churches.

Mr. Lincoln's Words.

The events of the year 1863 were enough to "harrow-up the souls" of all lovers of the glorious Republic. Abraham Lincoln was President, Horatio Seymour Governor and William G. Fargo Mayor of Buffalo. Among the Aldermen that year were Jacob Scheu, Lewis P. Dayton, Nelson K. Hopkins, Col. Rodney M. Taylor, Paul Goembel, John Hanavan, Elijah Ambrose, Jacob Crowder, Robert Mills, S. D. Cole, Charles Beckwith, O. C. Hoyt, George B. Gates. Many of these men still survive. Buffalo had a "War Committee" then of 13 members, only two of whom survive: Joseph L. Haberstro and Henry Nanert.

In his fervent, almost pathetic proclamation designating Thursday, November 26, as a day for Thanksgiving in 1863, Mr. Lincoln said: "I recommend to all, that while offering up their ascriptions justly due to Him for such singular deliverances and blessings, they do also, with humble penitence for our perverseness and disobedience, commend to His tender care all those who have become widows, orphans, mourners or sufferers in the lamentable civil strife in which we are unavoidably engaged, and fervently implore the interposition of the Almighty's hand to heal the wounds of the Union and to restore it as soon as may be consistent with the Divine purposes to the full enjoyment of peace, harmony and prosperity."

No less eloquent and earnest was the petition of the patriotic Seymour. He said, in part: "In the midst of calamities brought upon our country by the wickedness, folly, and crimes of men, we have reason to be thankful to Almighty God for abundant harvests, for exemption from pestilence, and for the preservation of our State from the devastations of war which afflict other sections of our land. Let us offer fervent prayers that Rebellion may be put down, our Union saved, our Liberties preserved, and our Constitution and Government upheld."

The Courier of Friday, November 27, 1863, says: "Buffalo enjoyed a quiet, old-fashioned Thanksgiving yesterday. The churches were attended in the forenoon by crowded audiences." Editors were too busy in those exciting times to devote much space to such services, so three lines sufficed for Thanksgiving, while columns were devoted to the doings of Grant and Sherman at Chattanooga, the army on the Rapidan, etc. From another source it is learned that collections were taken up in all of the churches, for the poor; also that donations were made to the Buffalo Army Committee of the United States Christian Commission, of clothing and supplies for the suffering troops at the front. It should be recalled now and here that that noble committee consisted of such good men as J. D. Hill, M. D.; J. F. Ernst, N. A. Halbert, O. F. Presbrey, Jason Sexton, F. Gridley, S. D. Sikes, S. H. Fish, and J. B. Sweet.

At 11 a. m. the various congregations of Presbyterians went to Dr. John C. Lord's Central Church and heard the eloquent preacher preach a vigorous war sermon. The Rev. J. B. Wentworth preached in the Pearl Street M. E. Church, and the Rev. J. H. Hartzell preached in the Universalist Church. Two events of importance occurred on the morning of November 25—an eclipse of the moon and the burning of old Fort Porter.

When "Johnnie came marching home" in 1865, after Lee's surrender, he gave thanks continuously, and President Johnson, after "Honest Abe" Lincoln's assassination, was so preoccupied with the cares of dissatisfied and dissatisfied Republicans—that he paid little attention to Thanksgiving Day.

The 29th day of November was designated by President Andrew Johnson and Governor Reuben E. Fenton as Thanksgiving Day in 1866. The soldiers of the Union had turned their swords into plowshares and the fruits of peace were being reaped by all sections of the reunited country. Fenian trials were in progress in Toronto. On the morning of Thanksgiving Day the bells of St. Paul's Church chimed "My Country 'Tis of Thee," "Hail Columbia," and "The Star Spangled Banner." The Presbyterians held union services in Calvary Church, with the Rev. Alexander McLean as preacher, and the Rev. D. H. Muller preached in Grace M. E. Church. Lotta was one of the theatrical attractions of the day.

War in Europe.

The fiery Frenchmen and Germans were having considerable fun on French soil in 1870, but the peace-loving Americans, on November 24, 1870, assembled in their churches—particularly in Buffalo—and gave thanks for many blessings. The Liedertafel gave a concert and ball on the preceding night and the Courier's critic said of the conductor: "The director, Mr. Joseph Mischka, will be found an earnest and conscientious worker and when he learns to curb his enthusiasm and demonstrativeness as a conductor, we shall have no fault to find with him." It was his first appearance as director. The soloists included Miss Fälsinger, Jennie Mann, Anna Mischka, Mr. Woehnert, and Mr. Rindemann. Bishop McQuaid of Rochester preached at St. Louis Church, the Rev. O. W. Witherspoon at Christ Church, Lucille Western was one of the footlight favorites that day.

The proclamation issued by President Grant and Governor John T. Hoffman designated Thursday, November 30, 1871, as Thanksgiving Day. Gen. Grant's proclamation was as brief as possible, and though it is paradoxical, Governor Hoffman's was even more condensed. It was a piercing cold, wintry day with plenty of snow. It was a great day for American "sports" for on that day, in Louisiana, Joe Coburn "stopped the best man in the world"—using his own words—by finishing Jem Mace in three hours and 38 minutes of hard fighting in the prize ring. But the referee called it a draw, saying in his own eloquent, classical way, "One is afraid and the other is afraider."

The attendance at the local churches was large. The Rev. Walcott Calkins, the Rev. Dr. Frothingham, the Rev. Dr. Heacock—now deceased—were the chief preachers of the day. The Board of Supervisors adjourned sine die on that day, and the chairman, Spencer Stone of Alden, was given a gold-headed cane by his colleagues. The address was made by Supervisor Albert Haight—now a Justice of the New York Court of Appeals. In the line of amusements that day, we had the "Vienna Lady Orchestra," Edwin Adams in "Enoch Arden," etc.

Death of Greeley.

A bright and pleasant holiday was Thanksgiving Day, November 29, 1872—the year of Gen. Grant's re-election over Horace Greeley. The distinguished journalist and humanitarian was a very sick man on Thanksgiving Day, and departed this life on the day following, lamented by the entire Nation. The newsboys and bootblacks of Buffalo were given a feast at Grace M. E. Church. The exercises of that occasion included addresses by ex-President Fillmore, Judge Clinton, W. P. Letchworth, James S. Lyon, and others. Rabbi Falk pronounced the benediction. The Courier employees gave a dance at Concert Hall. Aimee' was a theatrical attraction.

The "feast of the street gamins" at St. James Hall was the principal part of the Thanksgiving celebration here on November 27, 1873. The proclamations of Gen. Grant and Governor Dix were read, the Hon. Asher P. Nichols, Bishop Coxe and others spoke and about 600 happy newsboys gorged themselves. The Beecher-Tilton scandal was the sensation of that epoch.

Buffalo. n.y. courier 11-24-95

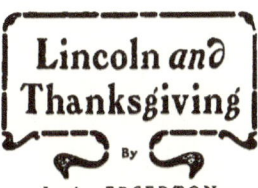

Lincoln and Thanksgiving

By

J. A. EDGERTON

LINCOLN GIVING THANKS.

LIKE so many other good things, Thanksgiving day in America originated with the Puritans. But in its present form as a national holiday it really owes its existence to Abraham Lincoln. The annual designation by the president of the last Thursday in November for such observance was started by him in 1863, and there has since been no break in the yearly Thanksgiving proclamations since that date.

The first Lincoln proclamation appointing a day for divine supplication was dated Aug. 12, 1861. It designated the last Thursday in September as "a day of humiliation, prayer and fasting." Things did not look especially bright for the northern arms just then. The memory of Bull Run was still fresh. Perhaps to this fact may be ascribed the pathetic wording of the document:

Whereas, When our own beloved country, once, by the blessing of God, united, prosperous and happy, is now afflicted with faction and civil war, it is peculiarly fit for us to recognize the hand of God in this terrible visitation and in sorrowful remembrance of our own faults and crimes as a nation and as individuals to humble ourselves before him and to pray for his mercy.

Thousands of individuals throughout the land refrained from food and prayed for the nation's salvation. The regular Thanksgiving in November, 1861, was a rather subdued occasion and there was no presidential proclamation. By the following spring, however, the clouds had begun to lift. Forts Henry and Donelson had been captured and Shiloh had been fought. So on the 10th of April Lincoln requested that the people give thanks because "it has pleased Almighty God to vouchsafe signal victories to the land and naval forces." Thanksgiving day proper in November of 1862 was observed much as it had been the year previous and no proclamation accompanied it.

The momentous year of 1863 saw three such proclamations, however. The first was dated March 30 and designated April 30 as a day of fasting and prayer. In this rather noteworthy document occurs the significant statement, "But we have forgotten God."

By July 15 Vicksburg had opened the Mississippi, and Gettysburg had ended the fear of invasion, so on that day another proclamation was issued, reciting that God had heard the prayers of the people and had vouchsafed "victories on land and sea so signal and so effective" as to promise ultimate peace. So Thursday, Aug. 6, was set apart as a day for national thanksgiving.

On Oct. 3 came the first of Lincoln's regular Thanksgiving day proclamations. It recites the brighter outlook for the Union, dwells lovingly on the continued growth of the nation despite its tribulations, gratefully points to the fact that other nations have not been drawn into the struggle, and says, "No human counsel hath devised nor hath any mortal hand worked out these great things," so the last Thursday in November is set apart as "a day of thanksgiving and praise."

July 7, 1864, by direction of congress, President Lincoln designated the first Thursday of August "as a day of national humiliation and prayer." Oct. 20 of the same year saw the issuance of Lincoln's second and last regular Thanksgiving proclamation. Before Thanksgiving day arrived it was known that Lincoln, by an overwhelming majority, had been chosen to succeed himself. The war was wearing to a close, and the occasion was auspicious.

IN TIME OF UNHAPPINESS

Facts About President Lincoln's Thanksgiving Proclamations During the War. *1911*

The initial date of the national Thanksgiving has been fixed at September 3, 1864, but this seems somewhat arbitrary. On April 10, 1862, (Nicolay & Hay, Complete Works, vii., 144), President Lincoln issued a proclamation recommending general thanksgiving and prayer for the national victories on the weekly day of religious observance next following the receipt of the proclamation. On July 15, 1863, (ix., 33) he issued a thanksgiving proclamation for victories and appointed Thursday, August 6, as the day of such observance. A second proclamation in the same year dated October 3, (ix., 151), in more general terms appointed the last Thursday in November as a day of thanksgiving and praise. On May 9, 1864, (x., 94), he issued a less formal 'recommendation of thanksgiving" without setting apart any day for observance. In the serial examinations of these records we now discover that the assignment of the initial date to September 3, 1864, is more than arbitrary, it is absurd. On that day President Lincoln issued two orders of thanks and rejoicing" (x., 213), tendering the national banks to Farragut, Canby and Granger and setting apart September 5, 6 and 7 for national salutes of 100 guns. On October 20, 1864, (x., 245), he issued his second thanksgiving proclamation for the last Thursday of November. These thanksgivings were a part of the war feeling. That they were continued after the war and were turned into more general channels is due to the success of the agitation carried on most earnestly by Sarah Josepha Hale, editor of Godey's Ladies' Book.

A COMMUNITY THANKSGIVING

Wausau wb. 11-27-14

The arrangement now practically completed, by
which the people of Wausau will unite in a community Thanksgiving service in one of the the-
aters of the city on Thursday, appeals alike to the
sense and the sentiment of people as a good way
to observe this peculiarly American holiday. A
community service of this character is undenomi-
national in every meaning of the word. It will be
open to everyone. Harry E. Dodge of Rochester,
New York, an interesting and spiritual speaker,
will deliver the principal address. Besides this,
there will be song services, and everything calculated to impress upon the minds and hearts of
those attending the true spirit of thanksgiving which
actuated Abraham Lincoln when he asked congress
to make the annual Thanksgiving Day a permanent institution in the United States, during the
trying period of the Civil war, as well as a token
of the feeling back to the early thanksgiving observances of the Pilgrim Fathers, and of the
American revolutionary soldiers during the war of
Independence.

It will be a splendid thing for Wausau if the
theater where the community Thanksgiving service
is held is filled to capacity Thursday. L. N. L.

LINCOLN LORE

Lincoln Lore
Bulletin of the
LINCOLN HISTORICAL RESEARCH
FOUNDATION
Dr. Louis A. Warren - Editor

This Bulletin is not copyrighted, but items used should be credited to The Lincoln National Life Insurance Co. Publishers.

LINCOLN'S THANKSGIVING PROCLAMATIONS

While we usually associate Thanksgiving Day, observed as early as 1621, with the family festivals of the Pilgrim Fathers, the origin of this national holiday is traced to the administration of Abraham Lincoln.

It would appear, from a study of the many proclamations of thanksgiving, fasting, and prayer issued by President Lincoln during the period of the Civil War, that no certain date could be established when the idea of an annual thanksgiving service first took form. On August 12, 1861, but five months after his inauguration, Lincoln issued a proclamation recommending "the last Thursday in September next as a day of humiliation, prayer and fasting for all the people of the Nation." On April 10, 1862, the people of the United States were invited to gather in their accustomed places of public worship at the next assembly to "render thanks" for victories won, "implore spiritual consolation" for the afflicted, and "invoke Divine guidance" for the National counsellors.

The year 1863 seems to have been accepted generally as the time when the idea of Thanksgiving took a more definite form. As early as the month of March the Senate of the United States requested the President "to designate and set apart a day for national prayer and humiliation." Lincoln "fully concurred in the views of the Senate" and issued a proclamation setting aside "April 30, 1863, as a day of national humiliation, fasting, and prayer."

On July 4, in announcing to the country the progress of the military activities, he requested that "on this day He whose will, not ours, should ever be done be everywhere remembered and reverenced with profoundest gratitude."

Eleven days after this announcement Lincoln issued another proclamation of thanksgiving for the victories of the Union forces, and set apart "Thursday, the sixth day of August next, to be observed as a day of national thanksgiving, praise, and prayer."

It was on October 3, 1863, that the proclamation influenced by the harvest season was issued, which may be considered more in harmony with the atmosphere surrounding the present observance of the day. This proclamation is printed here in full.

Proclamation for Thanksgiving
October 3, 1863

The year that is drawing toward its close has been filled with the blessings of fruitful fields and healthful skies. To these bounties, which are so constantly enjoyed that we are prone to forget the source from which they come, others have been added, which are of so extraordinary a nature that they cannot fail to penetrate and soften the heart which is habitually insensible to the ever-watchful providence of almighty God.

In the midst of a civil war of unequaled magnitude and severity, which has sometimes seemed to foreign states to invite and provoke their aggressions, peace has been preserved with all nations, order has been maintained, the laws have been respected and obeyed, and harmony has prevailed everywhere, except in the theater of military conflict; while that theater has been greatly contracted by the advancing armies and navies of the Union.

Needful diversions of wealth and of strength from the fields of peaceful industry to the national defense have not arrested the plow, the shuttle, or the ship; the ax has enlarged the borders of our settlements, and the mines, as well of iron and coal as of the precious metals, have yielded even more abundantly than heretofore. Population has steadily increased, notwithstanding the waste that has been made in the camp, the siege, and the battle-field, and the country, rejoicing in the consciousness of augmented strength and vigor, is permitted to expect continuance of years with large increase of freedom.

No human counsel hath devised, nor hath any mortal hand worked out these great things. They are the gracious gifts of the most high God, who, while dealing with us in anger for our sins, hath nevertheless remembered mercy.

It has seemed to me fit and proper that they should be solemnly, reverently, and gratefully acknowledged as with one heart and one voice by the whole American people. I do, therefore, invite my fellow-citizens in every part of the United States, and also those who are at sea and those who are sojourning in foreign lands, to set apart and observe the last Thursday of November next as a day of thanksgiving and praise to our beneficent Father who dwelleth in the heavens. And I recommend to them that, while offering up the ascriptions justly due to him for singular deliverances and blessings, they do also, with humble penitence for our national perverseness and disobedience, commend to his tender care all those who have become widows, orphans, mourners, or sufferers in the lamentable civil strife in which we are unavoidably engaged, and fervently implore the interposition of the almighty hand to heal the wounds of the nation, and to restore it, as soon as may be consistent with the Divine purposes, to the full enjoyment of peace, harmony, tranquility and union.

In testimony, etc.
    A. Lincoln.
By the President:
  William H. Seward,
   Secretary of State.

On three occasions, at least, in 1864, May 9, July 7, and September 3, the President issued proclamations in honor of victories achieved by the army.

The opening sentence of the proclamation of October 20, 1864, implies that Lincoln was thinking in the terms of an annual Thanksgiving Day.

Proclamation for Thanksgiving
October 20, 1864

It has pleased almighty God to prolong our national life another year, defending us with his guardian care against unfriendly designs from abroad, and vouchsafing to us in his mercy many and signal victories over the enemy, who is of our own household. It has also pleased our heavenly Father to favor as well our citizens in their homes, our soldiers in their camps, and our sailors on the rivers and seas, with unusual health. It has largely augmented our free population by emancipation and by immigration, while he has opened to us new sources of wealth, and has crowned the labor of our working-men in every department of industry with abundant rewards. Moreover, he has been pleased to animate and inspire our minds and hearts with fortitude, courage, and resolution sufficient for the great trial of civil war into which we have been brought by our adherence as a nation to the cause of freedom and humanity, and to afford to us reasonable hopes of an ultimate and happy deliverance from all our dangers and afflictions.

Now, therefore, I, Abraham Lincoln, President of the United States, do hereby appoint and set apart the last Thursday of November next as a day which I desire to be observed by all my fellow-citizens, wherever they may then be, as a day of thanksgiving and praise to Almighty God, the beneficent Creator and Ruler of the universe. And I do further recommend to my fellow-citizens aforesaid, that on that occasion they do reverently humble themselves in the dust, and from thence offer up penitent and fervent prayers and supplications to the great Disposer of events for a return of the inestimable blessings of peace, union and harmony throughout the land which it has pleased him to assign as a dwelling-place for ourselves and for our posterity throughout all generations.

In testimony, etc.
    Abraham Lincoln.
By the President:
  William H. Seward,
   Secretary of State.

To the Editor of The Courier-Journal.

In 1863 President Lincoln issued a proclamation for Thanksgiving Day. Since then every President has repeated it. But Thanksgiving Day had been more or less observed 242 years, or since the Pilgrims.

It would be just as near the truth to say that Lincoln started Thanksgiving Day as it would to leave the impression with the public that Constantine was the one who changed worship from Saturday to Sunday. Constantine simply became a convert of Christianity, and issued a proclamation, using the great power of his office to establish the Christian's day of worship; a day which they had observed since the resurrection of Christ. Except for the vast impetus given it by the great influence of his office, Constantine had no more to do with establishing Sunday as a day of worship than Lincoln had in originating Thanksgiving.

I might be elected as dictator, and then issue a proclamation establishing Mother's Day, but Mother's Day has already been observed for some time, therefore, my act would not make me the originator of it. When Constantine was converted to Christianity, it is perfectly natural that he would want to do something for it, so the biggest thing he saw that he could do at the moment was to declare for the Christian's Sabbath.

The fact that the Spirit-led disciples began to observe the First day is evidence that they recognized the Sabbath idea as a principle involving one-seventh of the time; not just a fixed segment of the week. Had they not recognized the principle rather than slavishness to a calendar day, then they would have been changing something that did not admit of change.

Louisville.   GEORGE SWANN.

LINCOLN LORE

Bulletin of the Lincoln National Life Foundation - - - - - - - - Dr. Louis A. Warren, Editor.
Published each week by The Lincoln National Life Insurance Company, of Fort Wayne, Indiana.

No. 294   **FORT WAYNE, INDIANA**   November 26, 1934

LINCOLN NATIONALIZES THANKSGIVING

Seasons of feasting and thanksgiving have been associated with the harvest season as long as food has been gathered and hoarded. The Pilgrims observed the harvest festival as a religious ceremony and largely determined the general characteristics of the feast as observed in America.

The domestic character of the thanksgiving idea retarded its national recognition, as usually it was confined to family, fraternal, or religious groups. Some of the states recognized the value of establishing a certain season for the festival, but it was not until the period of the Civil War that the national significance of the day was developed. A good picture of its nationalization is found in the following editorial of 1868:

"It is a fortunate circumstance that our national thank-offering festival has become a national affair in which the whole people participate upon a common day. This community of thanksgiving is due to the war and shows how firmly that struggle has bound together the different sections of our country. We forget that we are states and come to offer tribute to God in our capacity as a nation. The festival thus becomes more significant not only in its altered character but in its larger suggestions and motives."

The proclamation issued by Abraham Lincoln on October 3, 1863, is usually considered the first official appeal for the annual observance of a national Thanksgiving Day on the last Thursday in November. The importance of this document warrants the reprinting of the proclamation in full.

PROCLAMATION FOR THANKSGIVING
October 3, 1863

The year that is drawing toward its close has been filled with the blessings of fruitful fields and healthful skies. To these bounties, which are so constantly enjoyed that we are prone to forget the source from which they come, others have been added, which are of so extraordinary a nature that they cannot fail to penetrate and soften the heart which is habitually insensible to the ever-watchful providence of almighty God.

In the midst of a civil war of unequaled magnitude and severity, which has sometimes seemed to foreign states to invite and provoke their aggressions, peace has been preserved with all nations, order has been maintained, the laws have been respected and obeyed, and harmony has prevailed everywhere, except in the theater of military conflict; while that theater has been greatly contracted by the advancing armies and navies of the Union. Needful diversions of wealth and of strength from the fields of peaceful industry to the national defense have not arrested the plow, the shuttle, or the ship; the ax has enlarged the borders of our settlements, and the mines, as well of iron and coal as of the precious metals, have yielded even more abundantly than heretofore. Population has steadily increased, notwithstanding the waste that has been made in the camp, the siege, and the battle-field, and the country, rejoicing in the consciousness of augmented strength and vigor, is permitted to expect continuance of years with large increase of freedom.

No human counsel hath devised, nor hath any mortal hand worked out these great things. They are the gracious gifts of the most high God, who, while dealing with us in anger for our sins, hath nevertheless remembered mercy.

It has seemed to me fit and proper that they should be solemnly, reverently, and gratefully acknowledged as with one heart and one voice by the whole American people. I do, therefore, invite my fellow-citizens in every part of the United States, and also those who are at sea and those who are sojourning in foreign lands, to set apart and observe the last Thursday of November next as a day of thanksgiving and praise to our beneficent Father who dwelleth in the heavens. And I recommend to them that, while offering up the ascriptions justly due to him for singular deliverances and blessings, they do also, with humble penitence for our national perverseness and disobedience, commend to his tender care all those who have become widows, orphans, mourners, or sufferers in the lamentable civil strife in which we are unavoidably engaged, and fervently implore the interposition of the almighty hand to heal the wounds of the nation, and to restore it, as soon as may be consistent with the Divine purposes, to the full enjoyment of peace, harmony, tranquility, and union.

In testimony whereof, I have hereunto set my hand, and caused the seal of the United States to be affixed.

Done at the city of Washington, this third day of October, in the year of our Lord one thousand eight hundred and sixty-three, and of the independence of the United States the eighty-eighth.

                        A. LINCOLN.

By the President: WILLIAM H. SEWARD, Secretary of State.

There are many other appeals addressed to the American people by Abraham Lincoln which reveal the attitude of the Chief Executive towards the vital elements which constitute a national day of thanksgiving. Although disconnected, they contribute to the atmosphere permeating the period in which our national observance first found expression.

Annual Message 12/6/1854

"Again the blessings of health and abundant harvest claim our profoundest gratitude to almighty God."

"It is fit and becoming in all people, at all times, to acknowledge and revere the supreme government of God; to bow in humble submission to his chastisements; to confess and deplore their sins and transgressions, in the full conviction that the fear of the Lord is the beginning of wisdom." *Proc. of Nat'l Fast Day 8/12/1861*

"We have been the recipients of the choicest bounties of Heaven. We have been preserved, these many years, in peace and prosperity. We have grown in numbers, wealth, and power as no other nation has ever grown; but we have forgotten God." *Proc. of Nat'l Fast Day 3/30/1863*

"I invite the people of the United States to assemble in their customary places of worship, and, in the forms approved by their own consciences, render the homage due to the Divine Majesty for the wonderful things he has done in the nation's behalf." *Proc. of Nat'l Fast Day 3/30/1863*

"Intoxicated with unbroken success, we have become too self-sufficient to feel the necessity of redeeming and preserving grace, too proud to pray to the God that made us." *Proc. of Nat'l Fast Day 3/30/1863*

"It is the duty of nations as well as of men to own their dependence upon the overruling power of God; to confess their sins and transgressions in humble sorrow, yet with assured hope that genuine repentance will lead to mercy and pardon; and to recognize the sublime truth, announced in the Holy Scriptures and proven by all history, that those nations only are blessed whose God is the Lord." *Proc. of Nat'l Fast Day 3/30/1863*

Lincoln Proclaimed Thanksgiving
Day for Nation in Midst of War

Ft. Wayne Journal-Gazette 11-29-34

A NEWSPAPER editor was one of the first to observe the significance of Thanksgiving as celebrated nationally for the first time on November 26, 1863, according to the Lincoln student, Dr. Louis A. Warren, historian of the Lincoln National Life Insurance company.

The editorial referred to appeared in "Harper's Weekly," an illustrated newspaper of the period, and said in part:

"It is a fortunate circumstance that our annual thank-offering festival has become a national affair in which the whole people participate upon a common day. . . . We forget that we are states and come to offer tribute to God in our capacity as a nation. The festival thus becomes more significant not only in its altered character but in its larger suggestions and motives."

Dr. Warren called attention to the fact that the final emancipation proclamation, the Gettysburg address, and the first national Thanksgiving proclamation all came from the pen of Lincoln during the year 1863. Gettysburg day preceded Thanksgiving day just one week.

The proclamation for Thanksgiving, issued October 3, 1863, follows:

Proclamation for Thanksgiving
October 3, 1863

The year that is drawing toward its close has been filled with the blessings of fruitful fields and healthful skies. To these bounties, which are so constantly enjoyed that we are prone to forget the source from which they come, others have been added, which are of so extraordinary a nature that they cannot fail to penetrate and soften the heart which is habitually insensible to the ever-watchful providence of Almighty God.

In the midst of a civil war of unequaled magnitude and severity, which has sometimes seemed to foreign states to invite and provoke their aggressions, peace has been preserved with all nations, order has been maintained, the laws have been respected and obeyed, and harmony has prevailed everywhere, except in the theater of military conflict; while that theater has been greatly contracted by the advancing armies and navies of the Union.

Needful diversions of wealth and of strength from the fields of peaceful industry to the national defense have not arrested the plow, the shuttle, or the ship; the ax has enlarged the borders of our settlements, and the mines, as well of iron and coal as of the precious metals, have yielded even more abundantly than heretofore. Population has steadily increased, notwithstanding the waste that has been made in the camp, the siege, and the battlefield, and the country, rejoicing in the consciousness of augmented strength and vigor, is permitted to expect continuance of years with large increase of freedom.

No human counsel hath devised, nor hath any mortal hand worked out these great things. They are the gracious gifts of the most high God, who, while dealing with us in anger for our sins, hath nevertheless remembered mercy.

It has seemed to me fit and proper that they should be solemnly, reverently, and gratefully acknowledged as with one heart and one voice by the whole American people. I do, therefore, invite my fellow-citizens in every part of the United States, and also those who are at sea and those who are sojourning in foreign lands, to set apart and observe the last Thursday of November next as a day of thanksgiving and praise to our beneficent Father who dwelleth in the heavens. And I recommend to them that, while offering up the ascriptions justly due to him for singular deliverances and blessings, they do also, with humble penitence for our national perverseness and disobedience, commend to his tender care all those who have become widows, orphans, mourners, or sufferers in the lamentable civil strife in which we are unavoidably engaged, and fervently implore the interposition of the almighty hand to heal the wounds of the nation, and to restore it, as soon as may be consistent with the divine purposes, to the full enjoyment of peace, harmony, tranquility, and union.

In testimony whereof, I have hereunto set my hand, and caused the seal of the United States to be affixed.

Done at the city of Washington, this third day of October, in the year of our Lord one thousand eight hundred and sixty-three, and of the independence of the United States the eighty-eighth.

A. LINCOLN,

By the President:

WILLIAM H. SEWARD,
Secretary of State.

Editor Was First To Note
Import Of Thanksgiving

News Sentinel 11-29-3

A newspaper editor was one of the first to observe the significance of Thanksgiving as celebrated nationally for the first time on November 26, 1863, according to Dr. Louis A. Warren, Lincoln student and historian of The Lincoln National Life Insurance Company.

The editorial referred to appeared in "Harper's Weekly," an illustrated newspaper of the period, and said in part:

"It is a fortunate circumstance that our annual thank-offering festival has become a national affair in which the whole people participate upon a common day . . . We forget that we are states and come to offer tribute to God in our capacity as a nation. The festival thus becomes more significant not only in its altered character but in its larger suggestions and motives."

Dr. Warren called attention to the fact that the final Emancipation Proclamation, the Gettysburg Address, and the first national Thanksgiving Proclamation all came from the pen of Lincoln during the year 1863. Gettysburg Day preceded Thanksgiving Day just one week.

The Proclamation for Thanksgiving, issued on October 3, 1863, follows:

"Proclamation For Thanksgiving.

"October 3, 1863.

"The year that is drawing toward its close has been filled with the blessings of fruitful fields and healthful skies. To these bounties, which are so constantly enjoyed that we are prone to forget the source from which they come, others have been added, which are of so extraordinary a nature that they cannot fail to penetrate and soften the heart which is habitually insensible to the ever-watchful providence of almighty God.

"In the midst of a civil war of unequaled magnitude and severity, which has sometimes seemed to foreign states to invite and provoke their aggressions, peace has been preserved with all nations, order has been maintained, the laws have been respected and obeyed, and harmony has prevailed everywhere, except in the theatre of military conflict; while that theatre has been greatly contracted by the advancing armies and navies of the Union.

"Needful diversions of wealth and of strength from the fields of peaceful industry to the national defense have not arrested the plow, the shuttle, or the ship; the ax has enlarged the borders of our settlements, and the mines, as well of iron and coal as of the precious metals, have yielded even more abundantly than heretofore. Population has steadily increased, notwithstanding the waste that has been made in the camp, the siege, and the battle-field, and the country, rejoicing in the consciousness of augmented strength and vigor, is permitted to expect continuance of years with large increase of freedom.

"No human counsel hath devised, nor hath any mortal hand worked out these great things. They are the gracious gifts of the most high God, who, while dealing with us in anger for our sins, hath nevertheless remembered mercy.

Asks Observance.

"It has seemed to me fit and proper that they should be solemnly, reverently, and gratefully acknowledged as with one heart and one voice by the whole American people. I do, therefore, invite my fellow-citizens in every part of the United States, and also those who are at sea and those who are sojourning in foreign lands, to set apart and observe the last Thursday of November next as a day of thanksgiving and praise to our beneficent Father who dwelleth in the heavens. And I recommend to them that, while offering up the ascriptions justly due to him for singular deliverances and blessings, they do also, with humble penitence for our national perverseness and disobedience, commend to his tender care all those who have become widows, orphans, mourners, or sufferers in the lamentable civil strife in which we are unavoidably engaged, and fervently implore the interposition of the almighty hand to heal the wounds of the Nation, and to restore it, as soon as may be consistent with the Divine purposes, to the full enjoyment of peace, harmony, tranquility, and union.

"In testimony whereof, I have hereunto set my hand, and caused the seal of the United States to be affixed.

"Done at the city of Washington, this third day of October, in the year of our Lord one thousand eight hundred and sixty-three, and of the independence of the United States the eighty-eighth.

"A. LINCOLN

"By the President: William H. Se-

Credits Lincoln, Not Puritans, with Thanksgiving Day

CAMBRIDGE, Mass., Nov. 28.— (UP)—It wasn't the Puritans but Abraham Lincoln who established Thanksgiving day.

A collection of rare Thanksgiving proclamations in the Harvard library reveals that the Puritans were likely to have Thanksgiving any time of the year. The custom persisted and in 1795 George Washington proclaimed Thanksgiving on February 19.

After the battle of Gettysburg, Lincoln made Thanksgiving a national holiday. His successor, Andrew Johnson, chose the last Thursday in November as the date.

LINCOLN LORE

Bulletin of the Lincoln National Life Foundation - - - - - - - Dr. Louis A. Warren, Editor.
Published each week by The Lincoln National Life Insurance Company, of Fort Wayne, Indiana.

Number 397   FORT WAYNE, INDIANA   November 16, 1936

TRIBUTES ON THANKSGIVING DAY—1863

Although seasons of thanksgiving and prayer had been observed in America from the very earliest days of its settlement, it was not until the year 1863, that the last Thursday in November was set apart as a national Thanksgiving Day to be observed annually.

We assume it would be of interest to learn just what people had to be thankful for in the midst of a great civil war. Some excerpts from contemporary papers will allow us to catch the spirit of the first National Thanksgiving Day.

Editorial in New York Herald

One of the most unique editorials appearing in the press of the day, appeared in *The New York Herald* for November 26, 1863. The editor chose from the proclamations of the President, Governors, and Mayors, excerpts, which were combined in a composite summary, not entirely free from sarcasm.

"There are a great many blessings for which the American people, or the loyal portion thereof, should this day return thanks to their Creator. With the President of the United States we think they should be thankful for fruitful fields and healthful skies and for Unicn victories. With the Governor of New York, we believe that citizens should make contributions for the comfort of those made destitute by the casualties of war. With the Mayor of the city of New York, we are grateful because the area of the rebellion has been circumscribed, and the spirit of anarchy subdued. We agree with the Mayor of the city of Brooklyn in praying that "the rebellion may be speedily suppressed, and the Union preserved." With the Governor of Maine, we are thankful that "so many of our oppressed countrymen have been delivered from the hands of a cruel and merciless enemy"—by means of the cartel of exchange of prisoners, we take to be his Excellency's meaning. With the Governor of Vermont, we agree thanks are due for the "suppression of the murderous spirit of riot and anarchy." With the Governor of Massachusetts, we pray that "peace shall soon return to our borders, and a union of hearts and hands revive on the ruins of that injustice and inhumanity which bred our sorrows"—although we cannot exactly make out to which side his Excellency of the Bay State particularly refers; but we object to "injustice and inhumanity" on any side. We agree with the Governors of Rhode Island and Illinois that we should be thankful because "we still have a country," and further, with the Governor of the latter State, that such a consummation has been brought about "in spite of foreign hatred and plotting treason." With the Governor of Connecticut, we are thankful for the "increasing evidence of the fidelity of the people to the government.". With the Governor of New Jersey, we pray that the Creator "will give wisdom to those in authority." With the Governor of Pennsylvania, we are thankful for the "crowning mercy by which the bloodthirsty and devastating enemy was driven from the soil" of that State. It saved much trouble and confusion upon the soil of the State of New York. With the Governor of West Virginia, we do not know but that we are tolerably grateful "for the establishment and organization of a separate Commonwealth" out of the Old Dominion. With the Governors of the States of Ohio, Indiana, Illinois, Iowa, Michigan, Wisconsin and Minnesota, we are thankful that those States are in a state of unexampled prosperity, notwithstanding the war. . . ."

Excerpts from Beecher's New York Sermon

"When the President's proclamation appointing this Thanksgiving day was received in England, the *London Times*, that weathercock of nations, made itself merry and scornful over the idea of giving thanks for anything in America in her present condition, and there is indeed little that would be likely to excite thanksgiving in the breasts of those to whom God has denied faith and conscience, but we find transcendant mercies mingling with our afflictions. Our night has been long, its hours dark, its dreams troubled, and its watch'ng most weary; but it has had its stars, and they have led on the morning whose twilight is on the hills. Our day is at hand, the nation is to live . . .

"We owe a great debt to God in our Chief Magistrate. He is wisely and surely pioneering the way of liberty to this nation. One man there was whom God's hand ordained to break our foreign bondage. If it were possible to honor one more than him whom God has ordained to break the bondage of a worse oppression in our land, then the second should be greater than the first; but joined together, one and inseparable, we shall hereafter hear the shouts of Washington and Lincoln, the fathers of their country. . . ." (Applause.)

Paragraphs from Rev. Furness' Philadelphia Address

"I do not know one that should be mentioned before the gift which the bounty of Heaven has bestowd upon us in the man who has been called at this momentous hour to occupy the highest place in the nation. If I recollect right, I believe on a former thanksgiving occasion (I think it was the first thanksgiving recommended by the President), I named the President himself as one of the blessings for which we were bound to give thanks. We have more reason to be thankful for him now than we had then . . . We cannot tell how much we owe to his indomitable patience, to his "incorrigible honesty," to that singular wisdom by which he has been guided, I think without his being aware of it himself, and by which, while studying always anxiously to observe to the utmost the constitutional limitations which he registered his oath in honor to observe, he has never left it scarcely for a moment to be doubted that all his personal aims, feelings and opinions were on the side of liberty for every man, woman and child on our soil. Never yet was imposed upon any man so difficult a problem as he has been called to solve, and never had such a problem so successful a solution. Never was the conflict of official and personal duties so well settled as it has been thus far by President Lincoln. . . ."

Lincoln Proclaimed First Nation Wide Thanksgiving

Recognizing the fact that many people in our school as well as others are not aware of the fact that the first Thanksgiving was celebrated as a result of the decree issued by President Lincoln. Miss George has made a strenuous effort and has succeeded in securing the copy of the original proclamation. Clifford Davis of this school, Mr. Starr of the Detroit Bell Telephone Co; Mr. Vanderverre, a Detroit attorney, Mrs. J. D. Black of Grosse Point; and Mr. John B. Ames of the Lincoln Life Insurance Co. of Detroit have all been instrumental in securing the copy of the original proclamation.

Abraham Lincoln proclaimed the first annual national Thanksgiving day in 1863 with the following proclamation:

"The year that is drawing toward its close has been filled with the blessings of fruitful fields and healthful skies. To these bounties, which are so constantly enjoyed that we are prone to forget the source from which they come, others have been added, which are of so extraordinary a nature that they cannot fail to penetrate and soften the heart which is habitually insensible to the ever-watchful providence of almighty God..

Continued on page three

In the midst of a civil war of unequalled magnitude and severity, which has sometimes seemed to foreign states to invite and provoke their aggressions, peace has been preserved with all nations, order has been maintained, the laws have been respected and obeyed, and harmony has prevailed everywhere, except in the theater of military conflict; while that theater has been greatly contracted by the advancing armies and navies of the Union.

Needful diversions of wealth and of strength from the fields of peaceful industry to the national defense have not arrested the plow, the shuttle, or the ship; the ax has enlarged the borders of our settlements, and the mines, as well of iron and coal as of the precious metals, have yielded even more abundantly than heretofore. Population has steadily increased, notwithstanding the waste that has been made in the camp, the siege, and the battlefield; and the country, rejoicing in the consciousness of augmented strength and vigor, is permitted to expect continuance of years with large increase of freedom.

No human counsel hath devised, nor hath any mortal hand worked out these great things. They are the gracious gifts of the Most High God, who, while dealing with us in anger for our sins, hath neverless remembered mercy.

It has seemed to me fit and proper that they should be solemnly, reverently, and gratefully acknowledged as with one heart and one voice by the whole American people. I do, invite my fellow-citizens in every part of the United States, and also those who are at sea and those who are sojourning in foreign lands, to set apart and observe the last Thursday of November next as a day of thanksgiving and praise to our beneficent Father who dwelleth in the heavens. And I recommend to them that while offering up the ascriptions justly due to him for singular deliverances and blessings, they do also with humble penitence for our national perverseness and disobedience, commend to his tender care all those who have become widows, orphans, mourners, or sufferers in the lamentable civil strife in which we are unavoidably en-

Continued on column two

gaged, and fervently implore the interposition of the almighty hand to heal the wounds of the nation, and to restore it, as soon as may be consistant with the Divine purposes, to the full enjoyment of peace, harmony, tranquility, and union.

In testimony whereof, I have hereunto set my hand, and caused the seal of the United States to be affixed.

Done at the city of Washington, this third day of October, in the year of our Lord one thousand eight hundred and sixty-three, and of the independence of the United States the eighty-eighth.

Abraham Lincoln

THANKSGIVING IN AMERICAN HISTORY.

Paw Paw, Mich., Nov. 25.—I have just read your excellent editorial entitled " The Day of Thanksgiving." I note an error, however, which I am taking the liberty of correcting. You state that " each President since 1864 has followed Lincoln, who that year, when certainty of success had not dissipated the fears of failure, by a proclamation turned the minds of citizens to thoughts of their great trial and hopes of final deliverance."

The implication is that this was the first of the Lincoln Thanksgiving proclamations.

Having just completed the manuscript of a book entitled " Thanksgiving Day" in preparation for the writing of which I have read every book and magazine article I could find on the subject of Thanksgiving, as well as every Thanksgiving proclamation of the Presidents and the continental congress, consulting original records, etc., I can speak with some assurance on the dates of Thanksgiving proclamations.

On July 15, 1863, Lincoln issued a proclamation setting aside Thursday, Aug. 6, as a day of thanksgiving.

On Oct. 3, 1863, Lincoln issued another Thanksgiving proclamation setting aside the last Thursday in November as a day of thanksgiving.

The next Thanksgiving proclamation of Lincoln was issued Oct. 20, 1864. He set apart the last Thursday, in November "as a day of thanksgiving."

Johnson's first proclamation was issued Oct. 28, 1865, and he set the date "the first Thursday of the following December."

I trust you will not consider this carping criticism. I am doing this simply because of my interest in getting the exact truth concerning historical matters.   H. RANDEL LOOKABILL.

Lincolns Ate First Thanksgiving Dinner in Indiana 121 Yr. Ago

LINCOLN CITY, Ind., Nov. 24.—(AP)—The Thomas Lincoln family sat down on the earthen floor of its new one-room cabin 121 years ago to a wild turkey dinner and gave thanks for a "safe journey" through the wilderness from Kentucky, a "new home and blessings."

There were no chairs, no table, Thomas Lincoln, carpenter, hadn't had time to make any furniture. He had been too busy building the cabin, so that he might move his wife and two children into more comfortable quarters than the "half face" camp in which they had been living.

So it was with Thanksgiving that the little family—Thomas, his wife, Nancy Hanks Lincoln, and their two children, Sarah, 9, and "Abe," 7—enjoyed its first Thanksgiving day in Indiana. The wild turkey, which Thomas had killed in the wilderness, was a treat. So were wheat cakes, because flour was scarce.

On the long, hard trip from Kentucky and in the days that followed, the Lincolns hadn't had much to eat except potatoes and dried fruits.

Abraham Lincoln, remembering the day well, told in later years how his father gave thanks for their "safe journey, new home and blessings" and asked "the Father of all to abide with us in our new home and give us peace."

Thanksgiving two years later found the cabin in sadness. The mother of the boy who was to become the Civil war president had died only a few weeks before at the age of 35. Her grave is just across a valley from the cabin site, now marked by a stone monument. The boy Abraham helped his father make the rude coffin in which they buried her.

A Week-End
with LINCOLN

By Honoré Morrow

THE autumn that followed the battle of Gettysburg was particularly full of dramatic events, which took place in and around the White House, but of which Mr. Lincoln was more the spectator than the god from the machine. And yet he was much more than spectator, for his was the ultimate authority which set the events in motion. To show what I mean, I have gathered together some typical days, following the battle of battles of Chattanooga and Chickamauga.

On a cold but starlit midnight, John Hay arrived at the Soldier's Home on the outskirts of Washington, where the President had tried to find a night's rest. Hay went at once to Mr. Lincoln's bedroom.

"The Secretary of War wants you to come at once to his office for a conference, sir!" the young man said.

The President sat up in bed, hair disheveled, eyes anxious. "What now, John!" His voice was husky with sleep.

"More news from Tennessee, Mr. Lincoln! It seems that General Rosecrans' defeat was more disastrous than we thought. Rosecrans has legged it for Chattanooga, leaving his army behind him."

"No!" shouted Lincoln, springing out of bed.

"I'm afraid it's true, sir," insisted the young man, dismally. "Secretary Stanton's own words were 'I know why they lost the battle! Rosecrans ran away from his fighting men and didn't stop for thirteen miles! You can't blame McCook. I'll admit he and Crittenden made pretty good time away from the fight, but Rosecrans beat them both!'"

Lincoln was pulling on his clothes, his face grim. "Stanton never sent for me this way before. Things must be pretty bad. Order my horse for me, John, will you?"

"I did, sir, as I came in. Secretary Stanton doesn't seem scared. He's mad; mad as—as Stanton!"

The President shook his head. The losses had been fearful at Chickamauga. Stanton's excitement had something to do with this, he was sure.

The two men didn't slacken rein until they reached the very steps of the War Office. Seward, the Secretary of State was there and Chase, Secretary of the Treasury, as well as Halleck, The General in Chief of the Army and McCallum, Superintendent of Military Transportation.

Stanton was chewing his beard and pacing the floor. "Rosecrans has got to be reinforced instantly," he shouted at the President. "I need your authority to get these fellows," jerking his head at the others, "to get these fellows to move."

"Burnside will be with him with 12,000 men in less than ten days," said Lincoln, seating himself beside Halleck on the sofa. "No other men can be spared."

"Ten days!" shouted Stanton. "Do you want to lose the whole of Tennessee? While Meade sits on his rump beside the Rapidan, refusing to pursue General Lee, we are losing the whole of Rosecrans' army, the Army of the Cumberland. I'll move 30,000 of them from Virginia to Tennessee, if you'll force these fellows to co-operate." He glared at the distinguished gentlemen seated about his office.

General Halleck gave a feeble squeak of protest and looked appealingly at Lincoln.

"It can't possibly be done, Mr. Stanton," declared Lincoln. "It's a physical impossibility."

"If you help, I can get thirty thousand seasoned troops from the Army of the Potomac over the mountains to Chattanooga, in five days," insisted Stanton.

"You can't get them to Washington in five days," grunted the President.

"Certainly not," agreed Halleck. "Nor to Chattanooga in less than thirty." The others nodded, eyes on the raging Secretary of War.

Stanton turned on McCallum. "If you're given supreme authority and abundant transportation, how long would it take you?"

"Seven days," replied McCallum, "with that proviso."

"Show me the map," said Lincoln.

The railroad man walked to the map, spread on Stanton's desk. The others crowded round him. "With supreme authority," began (Continued on page 54)

(Continued from page 33)

McCallum and he proceeded to outline his plan. Lincoln whose heart had been wrung for two years by the apparently insuperable difficulty of moving Union troops rapidly—with even half the rapidity with which Confederate armies were moved—began in spite of himself to be impressed. McCallum and Stanton made a great team. Their scheme was well worth trying. He gave them the authority they needed and went over to the White House for a few hours rest.

He was greeted in the morning by word of his brother-in-law's death, of wounds got at Chickamauga. He was Mary's brother, a Confederate. Mary was in New York and Lincoln telegraphed the news to her and was beginning a letter to Rosecrans when Seward, the Secretary of State, rushed in.

"Mr. Lincoln," Seward began at once, "the Minister to England has pledged the word of this government that $10,000,000 in U. S. bonds shall be sent to London by the first steamer leaving New York after his request is received by the State Department here. The first steamer leaves New York on Monday and this is Friday."

"Great Jupiter! Is he buying those ironclads the British are building for the Confederates?" demanded Lincoln.

"He could send me only a few lines to catch the mail," explained Seward. "He says that if the British government orders the builders not to let those ironclads sail, they risk a huge suit for damages. But they will issue that order, pending investigation, if the United States will secure the damages by the deposit of $10,000,000 in gold coin. He had to act instantly. Of course, he had no such sum, and the cable isn't working. But it seems an anonymous Englishman voluntarily deposited the sum. Adams has pledged his immediate return by you—that is, by our Treasury."

Lincoln came slowly to his feet. The notorious case of the ironclads had made war with England imminent. The two men stared at each other while the significance of this anonymous gesture sank into Lincoln's mind. "Have you sent word to the Treasury?"

"Mr. Chase is following me here," replied Seward. "And here he is."

The Secretary of the Treasury came in, and after greeting the President, he said, "It can't be done if we must be ready Monday. Did you telegraph the steamer to delay a day or so?"

"Yes, but it's an English ship and has to have its orders from London. The cable isn't working. They leave Monday noon with or without our bonds," replied Seward.

"Explain yourselves, gentlemen!" demanded Lincoln.

"I have brought the Register of the Treasury for that very purpose," Chase said. "Will you call him, please."

The Register, V. E. Chittenden, a Vermont lawyer came in. Lincoln greeted him affectionately. The Register was a friend of his.

Chittenden began by stating that the problem was unique in the history of the Treasury. The sum of $10,000,000 must be made up by filling in, signing and sealing the bonds on hand, which were of small denominations. There was no time to print others. This meant that 12,500 bonds must be signed before four o'clock Monday morning.

"We must either put off the time for sailing or the President must appoint you two or three assistants," declared Mr. Chase.

The President shook his head. "Minister Adams had some reason, legal or otherwise, for stipulating a certain time of sailing. We dare do nothing but live up to the demand. As for appointing persons to sign with the Register, that also is illegal. What's your record on speed, Mr. Chittenden?"

"I've done two to three thousand in a day—very exhausting it is, even when I write my name with a single movement of the pen. Ten signatures to the minute. But this has got to be done. I have something over sixty hours, if I take no time off for rest or sleep. You can see I've not a second to spare!"

He bowed himself out of the office.

Lincoln waited a moment to hear Chase and Seward agree that it couldn't be done. Then he went over to Stanton's office to see if the troops were moving. Stanton hadn't slept for twenty-four hours and he was as cross as a mangy dog. Troops from the Rapidan, he shouted to the President, would be entering Washington within ten hours to entrain on the B. & O. for Tennessee. Every half hour a fresh train would start, not to stop except for wood and water. At these halts, the commissary department would supply hot food to the soldiers, who never were to leave their cars en route.

The President listened, patted Stanton's shoulder, signed whatever documents were necessary, sent a telegram to Rosecrans and to Grant and returned to his own office. At two o'clock he went over to the Treasury Building.

Three clerks, an army surgeon and a negro employee were grouped around Chittenden. One clerk counted out bonds in groups of ten. Another slid the ten under his right hand. The third removed the signed bond the instant the pen was raised.

"Need you work so continuously?" asked the President.

"It's easier so," replied the surgeon. "His fingers stiffen if he pauses."

"Well, all the soldiers aren't in the army!" ejaculated Lincoln. Then realizing it was cruel to distract Chittenden's attention, he stood in silence by the window, watching. The flies were fearful, for the cold air was driving them into shelter. The Negro, Lewis, used a palm leaf to keep them off the Register. Lincoln sighed. What superb effort! Stanton and his soldiers. Chittenden and his bonds. Tennessee and Virginia black with dead Americans. And all, all unnecessary! All waste! All loss! And he, Abraham Lincoln, butcher-in-chief. Surely, surely war was not the only way!

Back to his office in the White House. The waiting room was packed with people waiting to see him. He finished with them about nine o'clock and settled to work on the speech he was to make at Gettysburg in November. He wrote a sentence and paused to think. When the fathers gave birth to the nation, could they have conceived that the North would have put into the field 800,000 men to fight the South? He dropped his pen, lifted his head to listen—the shuffling beat of marching me *(incomplete,*

Reading — — — 193?

LINCOLN LORE

Bulletin of the Lincoln National Life Foundation - - - - - Dr. Louis A. Warren, Editor,
Published each week by The Lincoln National Life Insurance Company, Fort Wayne, Indiana

Number 503   FORT WAYNE, INDIANA   November 28, 1938

BY-PRODUCTS OF THE GETTYSBURG BATTLE

Lincoln's Gettysburg Address, delivered on November 19, 1863, preceeded by just one week the first annual Thanksgiving Day. Indirectly the Battle of Gettysburg was responsible for both the famous oration and the rather obscure but impressive proclamation by Lincoln.

Frequently the value of by-products, resulting from industrial enterprise, far exceeds the commodity for which the original project was planned. As a parallel in our national life it appears as if the by-products of the Gettysburg battle will eventually over-shadow the battle itself.

An elaborate program, commemorating the seventy-fifth anniversary of the battle, was sponsored by the government this past summer; but the two equally important by-products, the dedicatory address and the Thanksgiving Proclamation, received little attention on their respective seventy-fifth anniversaries.

Abraham Lincoln had been in office but a few days over five months when he issued his first proclamation for a day "of public prayer, humiliation, and fasting" to be observed on "the last Thursday in September", 1861. On April 10, 1862 he issued a Proclamation of Thanksgiving for victories of the army and for divine guidance.

During the year 1863 proclamations setting apart days of praise and prayer were issued on three occasions. A national fast day was appointed for the last Thursday in April, and on the first Thursday in August the people were called upon to "invoke the Holy Spirit to subdue the anger which has produced and so long sustained a needless and cruel rebellion".

Immediately after the Battle of Gettysburg, Sarah Josepha Hale wrote to President Lincoln appealing to him to set apart a day of Thanksgiving. Whether the Thanksgiving Proclamation which he issued on July 15, two weeks after the battle, setting aside August 6 as a day of Thanksgiving, or whether the proclamation of October 3, setting aside the last Thursday in November as a day of Thanksgiving, was the result of Mrs. Hale's appeal is problematical; but it is safe to say that both proclamations were inspired more or less by the military contest.

Mrs. Hale should be commended for her perseverance in attempting to have Thanksgiving Day observed annually throughout the nation, but she is not the parent of this annual festival as it is now observed, although she had advocated the day of thanks as early as 1827, and subsequently appealed to congress to establish an annual festival. It was not until Abraham Lincoln came to the White House that she succeeded in securing a favorable response. With all due respect to the Pilgrims, George Washington, James Madison, and Mrs. Hale in their respective contributions to the Thanksgiving tradition, it was Abraham Lincoln who became the founder of the annual national Thanksgiving celebration as we now observe it. Not only did he issue and sign the first proclamation in 1863, but he also emphasized the annual aspect of the celebration by issuing another Thanksgiving proclamation for 1864.

The second paragraph of the first annual national Thanksgiving Proclamation observes that "In the midst of a civil war of unequaled magnitude and severity . . .

the theatre of military conflict has been . . . greatly contracted by the advancing armies and navies of the Union". The third paragraph emphasizes "the waste that has been made in camp, the siege, and the battle field", and then Lincoln commends to God "all those who have become widows, orphans, mourners or sufferers in the lamentable civil strife".

The address delivered by Lincoln at the dedication of the Gettysburg Cemetery resulted, directly of course, from the Gettysburg battle. In the second paragraph of this address Lincoln recalls that "we are engaged in a great civil war" and that "we have met on a great battle-field of that war".

It may be observed from the references to the war that the Gettysburg battle was fresh in Lincoln's mind at the time the proclamation was issued, and, after all, it may indirectly have had about as much to do with the final issuing of the Thanksgiving Proclamation as any other influence.

Aside from the military aspects of both the Thanksgiving Proclamation and the Gettysburg Address, it is evident that the latter borrowed something in the way of diction from the less famous proclamation when Lincoln said "It is altogether fitting and proper that we should do this". He felt the same way about the proclamation and wrote, "It has seemed to me fit and proper", etc.

It might be truly said that the Gettysburg Address was written in the atmosphere of the Thanksgiving Proclamation and that both of these remarkable papers came out of the aftermath of the Gettysburg battle. The following brief excerpts reveal the same beauty of expression:

From the (Thanksgiving) Proclamation

"The year that is drawing toward its close has been filled with the blessings of fruitful fields and healthful skies. To these bounties, which are so constantly enjoyed that we are prone to forget the source from which they come, others have been added, which are of so extraordinary a nature that they cannot fail to penetrate and soften the heart which is habitually insensible to the ever-watchful providence of almighty God. . . .

"No human counsel hath devised, nor hath any mortal hand worked out these great things. They are the gracious gifts of the most high God, who, while dealing with us in anger for our sins, hath nevertheless remembered mercy."

From the Gettysburg Address

"It is rather for us to be here dedicated to the great task remaining before us,—that from these honored dead we take increased devotion to that cause for which they gave the last full measure of devotion—that we here highly resolve that these dead shall not have died in vain—that this nation, under God, shall have a new birth of freedom —and that government of the people, by the people, for the people, shall not perish from the earth".

THE COLLECTOR.
A Magazine for Autograph and Historical Collectors

Vol. LIII, No. 11   NEW YORK, SEPTEMBER, 1939   WHOLE No. 582

The Collector, Established 1887, is published the first day of the month. It will be sent, postpaid, One Year for One Dollar.

Address—

WALTER R. BENJAMIN
MARY A. BENJAMIN
655 Fifth Avenue

Telephone Plaza 8-3287   **NEW YORK CITY**

Vol. LIII   SEPTEMBER, 1939   No. 11

In the July issue of THE COLLECTOR, we made a plea to have our customers write bits for us on subjects of interest to them covering autograph or historical matters. As a result, several answered and have sent in splendid articles. The one below, written by Mr. H. S. J. Sickel, a distinguished member of the Philadelphia bar, was to have appeared in our columns in the November issue. Because of its timeliness, we print it now, without comment, feeling that our readers cannot fail to be interested. In sending the article Mr. Sickel stated: *"I have spent a lot of time on this subject, in reading, research and writing. To collect a copy of all the National Thanksgiving Proclamations alone was really a big job, but I am more than satisfied with my accomplishments, for, having done so, I have very good reason to believe that I am the only person who has a full and complete set (copy) of all the National Thanksgiving Proclamations, which have been issued in the United States. The whole subject to me has been one round of pleasure, and it is an additional pleasure to give you the benefit of some of my labors."*

THE THANKSGIVING TRADITION

The Pilgrim Fathers, their landing at Plymouth Rock and their Thanksgiving Service on December 20, 1620, are the fundamentals upon which we base our thoughts of Thanksgiving in the general belief that from these facts the holiday was developed. Such is not the case, however, for Thanksgiving and the practice of it are centuries old.

The first recorded references to it are found in the Old Testament, beginning with the early history of the Jewish people. With them Thanksgiving was a real event, and they repeatedly made use of it. It was not so much a question of seasons, although they annually gave thanks for crops garnered in harvest, as an occasion prompted by events happening in their sacred or secular history. As a result, their observance of the day was always associated with a ritual. Sometimes the ceremonies would last not only a day, but several days, and occasionally stretched over a period of a week or more. Usually they involved the making of gifts to God, the Priest or Temple-giving with sacrifices, fasting, feasting, song and prayer, humiliation and adoration.

The Jews were undoubtedly the originators of Thanksgiving and developed it in their usage and practice to a very high degree. But the earliest Christians were not slow in following their example and adopting it, for it was wholly harmonious with their own doctrine and religious philosophy. With the spread of Christianity westward, this particular custom came down through the centuries in different lands, to be practiced in individual and local ways. It finally became established in the Netherlands, where the people, during their eighty years war against the sovereignty of Spain, used it as an occasion on which to show their gratitude to the Almighty for their victories over the invaders. The famous hymn, *The Prayer of Thanksgiving*, of Holland Dutch origin, first sung in the 16th Century, has survived to the present day, and is still in use by the people of many nations, who are lovers of music and song.

The Pilgrim Fathers were of English birth and of different traditions. To them Thanksgiving was either an unknown event or not recognized. It was not until, separating from the Church of England because of their religious beliefs and departing for the New World, via Holland, where they remained for several years, that they became aware of other customs than their own. Particularly acceptable to them, as they fled religious oppression and saw freedom ahead, was Thanksgiving and its philosophy. It was a custom they did not forget, but on the contrary soon put in practice.

After sailing from Delft for America and enduring a long and hazardous journey across the Atlantic, their first thought upon landing at Plymouth Rock, Mass., on that cold December 20, 1620, and their first religious act, was to offer up a heartfelt prayer of Thanksgiving to God for their safe passage. Spring saw their number gravely depleted, for many had perished during the hard winter, but those who remained, undaunted in spirit, planted seed to provide the survivors with food for the new winter to come. When the autumn brought a rich harvest, their grateful leader, William Bradford, informally proclaimed a Thanksgiving Service to thank God for the continued existence of the Colony and for the crops they had gathered.

So the custom found its way to the Western Hemisphere, and became a tradition among these people and their descendants. As the number of Colonies grew and spread, it became the usage in all the New England Provinces, locally, through their civic leaders, to fix a certain day for Thanksgiving and to announce it by formal Proclamation. This day was religiously observed.

The first known and earliest existing formal Proclamation for Thanksgiving is that which was issued by the Council of the Town of Charlestown, Mass., June 20, 1676, appointing June 29, 1676, "as a day of solemn thanksgiving and praise to God for such His goodness and favor. . . ." In this Proclamation, the Council commended it "to the respective Ministers, Elders, and people of this Jurisdiction, solemnly and seriously to keep the same."

That Thanksgiving became a National holiday by virtue of President George Washington's Proclamation in 1789 is generally believed but is not the case. The first National Thanksgiving Proclamation in this Country was issued by the Continental Congress on November 7, 1777, recommending Thursday, December 18, 1777, as the appointed day. This act of the Continental Congress may well be accounted for by the fact that being made up in large part of delegates from the New England Colonies, their influence undoubtedly carried weight. These members not only came to this Congress with their well-established convictions on the questions of Government, Liberty and Independence, but they also carried with them their long-established philosophy of life in general, supplemented by deep religious beliefs.

It was natural then for Samuel Adams, Signer of the Declaration of Independence for Massachusetts, and his New England associates to offer a Resolution that a Committee of three be appointed to prepare a recommendation to the several States to set apart a day for Thanksgiving "for the signal successes lately obtained over the enemy of these United States." (The defeat of Burgoyne at Saratoga.) That Resolution was adopted, and Adams, Richard Henry Lee, the Virginia Signer, and Col. Daniel Roberdeau of Pennsylvania were duly appointed the Committee for that purpose. They drafted the proposed Proclamation, and it was subsequently considered and adopted.

The practice of issuing a formal National Proclamation for Thanksgiving, having once been started, was continued by the Continental Congress annually until and including the year 1783. Five years then followed in which no day was set aside. But in 1789 Washington issued his first National Thanksgiving Proclamation, suggested by and requested of him by Congress under the new Constitution. Both Houses by their joint Committee, on resolution authorizing the same, requested the President "to recommend to the people of the United States a day of public thanksgiving and prayer to be observed by acknowledging with grateful hearts the many signal favors of Almighty God, especially by affording them an opportunity peaceably to establish a form of Government for their safety and happiness." This first Presidential Proclamation, issued by Washington on October 3, 1789, recommended and appointed Thursday, November 26, 1789, the last Thursday of the month, as the day for National Thanksgiving.

The next Proclamation was not issued by Washington until January 1, 1795. At this time Thursday, February 19, 1795, was appointed the day of National observance. This Proclamation was issued by Washington on his own initiative. Following Washington, President John Adams issued two Proclamations; the first dated March 23, 1798, recommending May 9, 1798, and the second and last, issued in 1799, appointing Thursday, April 25, 1799.

President Thomas Jefferson, not believing in Thanksgiving, as he considered it too suggestive of a monarchy, issued no Proclamations. His successor, President James Madison, however, resumed the custom on joint resolution of Congress. His first Proclamation was dated November 16, 1814, and appointed Thursday, January 12, 1815. His second and last Proclamation, dated March 4, 1815, appointed Thursday, April 13, 1815.

With this last Proclamation issued by President Madison, the practice of a National Thanksgiving, with a Proclamation therefor, was discontinued for exactly forty-seven years, to the day. It was not revived until President Lincoln, at his own instance, issued a Proclamation, dated April 10, 1862, appointing Sunday, April 13, 1862, a day for National Thanksgiving.

While Lincoln, on joint resolution of Congress, by resolution of the Senate, and on concurrent resolution of Congress issued three Proclamations for National humiliation, fasting and prayer in 1861, 1863, and 1864, respectively, and before him on December 14, 1860, President James Buchanan had issued a similar Proclamation, on the special appeal of many, the credit for reviving the custom of Thanksgiving must go to L[...]. During his administration, we find [...] not only reinstated the National obse[...] of the day, but it was by, by his thi[...] fourth Proclamations, in 1863 and 186[...] following Washington's example, app[...] the last Thursday of November as [...] for National Thanksgiving. This precedent that has been followed religiously each and every succeeding Preside[...] nually, with two exceptions. In 1865, President Andrew Johnson appointed Thu[...] December 7, and in 1869, President U[...] S. Grant appointed Thursday, Novemb[...] the respective dates. In 1870, Pre[...] Grant reverted to the last Thursd[...] November as the annual custom and [...] date by custom, precedent and use has[...] appointed by all succeeding President[...] has become well established as the tim[...] our National Thanksgiving.

Thanksgiving is not a National Legal day; it is really a Holy-day, although ordered or decreed as such by the Ch[...] It has not only a religious but a se[...] background, confirmed by legal autho[...] Thanksgiving technically may be defined National Anniversary, having sanctio[...] antiquity, with the approbation of ou[...] ligious convictions, confirmed by usage[...] custom, and definitely fixed upon the se[...] calendar.

The reading and study of each and e[...] one of these National Proclamations [...] 1777 to date will reveal that they are [...] velous pieces of English literature, teem[...] with religious fervor, containing refere[...] to outstanding events, historical, econom[...] governmental, and domestic, in the histo[...] this Country. In many instances they [...] expression of thought coming from [...] depths of the soul of their authors, the P[...] dents of the United States. Together [...] are an imposing record of the Nations' [...] standing events and are well worth read[...] Thanksgiving has unquestionably develo[...] into one of the institutions of our Ame[...] life.

H. S. J. SICKE[...]

FIRST PROCLAMATION OF THANKSGIVING, AS WRITTEN BY BRADFORD

The first Thanksgiving proclamation was made by Gov. William Bradford of the Massachusetts Bay colony three years after the Pilgrims settled at Plymouth Rock. It established the first Thanksgiving as Nov. 29, 1623. The text of the porclamation follows:

TO ALL YE PILGRIMS:

"Inasmuch as the Great Father has given us this year an abundant harvest of Indian corn, wheat, peas, beans, squashes, and garden vegetables, and has made the forests to abound with game and the sea with fish and clams, and inasmuch as he has protected us from the ravages of the savages, has spared us from pestilence and disease, has granted us freedom to worship God according to the dictates of our own conscience; now I, your magistrate, do proclaim that all ye Pilgrims, with your wives and ye little ones, do gather at ye meethouse, on ye hill, between the hours of 9 and 12 in the day time, on Thursday, November ye 29th, of the year of our Lord one thousand six hundred and twenty-three, and the third year since ye Pilgrims landed on ye Plymouth Rock, there to listen to ye pastor and render thanksgiving to ye Almighty God for all his blessings.

"WILLIAM BRADFORD,
"Ye Governor of Ye Colony."

Chicago Tribune 11-23-39

LINCOLN·LORE

Bulletin of the Lincoln National Life Foundation - - - - - - Dr. Louis A. Warren, Editor,
Published each week by The Lincoln National Life Insurance Company, Fort Wayne, Indiana

Number 555 FORT WAYNE, INDIANA November 27, 1939

A LINCOLN MEMORIAL TO THANKSGIVING

There are several heroic bronze statues in America which memorialize important events or episodes in the life of Abraham Lincoln. The Hoosier Youth, The Rail-splitter, Captain Lincoln, The Circuit Rider, The Debater, The Emancipator, The Orator at Gettysburg, and The Lincoln of the Second Inaugural Address are some of the themes visualized by these bronze figures.

Sometimes the environment of a statue contributes much to the message which the figure conveys. It was appropriate indeed to place the statue of Lincoln the Debater in one of the towns where Lincoln engaged Douglas in debate; to locate Lincoln the Circuit Rider in a county seat of the old Eight Judicial Districts; to erect at Washington, D. C., the famous Ball statue of Lincoln the Emancipator.

There has recently been dedicated at Hingham, Massachusetts, an heroic bronze statue by Charles Keck, which might well serve as a bronze memorial to the first annual national proclamation of Thanksgiving issued by Abraham Lincoln in 1863. Certainly no other community in New England could offer such a favorable environment for a Lincoln memorial to Thanksgiving. In this festival are blended the atmosphere of the family circle, the deep religious sentiment of the Puritans, the spirit of patriotism which dominate'd the fathers, and the harvest environment.

Thanksgiving is our outstanding family festival. Hingham has been a Lincoln family settlement for more than three hundred years; there is no town in America so predominantly Lincoln. As early as 1637 there were eight men living in Hingham by the name of Lincoln; no other family group was represented by so many adult males. Their sons played a prominent part in the colonial history of New England, one author naming 350 prominent men with Lincoln blood in their veins. As late as 1854 there were twenty-three men by the name of Lincoln on the list of legal voters residing in Hingham, and the name is by no means uncommon there today. It is appropriate indeed that the bronze statue of Abraham Lincoln should face the building site where Samuel Lincoln, the first American progenitor of President Lincoln, established his home. In the very shadow of the statue seven generations of Samuel Lincoln's descendants were reared.

A festival of Thanksgiving which is primarily religious would find a congenial atmosphere in a town such as Hingham where there is a pronounced spiritual sentiment. Here there is located the Old Ship Church, used continuously for religious worship longer than any other church structure standing in America today. Samuel Lincoln was a member of this congregation and one of the builders of the original edifice. When Abraham Lincoln issued his memorable Thanksgiving Proclamation, Calvin Lincoln, a kinsman, was the minister of the Hingham church.

Patriotism was a cardinal virtue with the colonial Lincolns and, with the exception of General Washington himself, no Revolutionary soldier stood higher in the esteem of the people than General Benjamin Lincoln of Hingham. There was an Abraham Lincoln, descendant of Samuel of Hingham, who took part in the seige of Boston on March 4, 1776. The Lincolns intermarried with the family of Paul Revere.

It was a happy thought to have the bronze statue of Lincoln at Hingham dedicated in the fall of the year with suggestions of the harvest season everywhere about, thus contributing to the surroundings of the occasion the final element to make them appropriate indeed. Family history, religious appeal, and patriotic shrines were blended into an ideal Thanksgiving atmosphere.

Shortly after Mr. Keck completed the original bronze study of Lincoln, the editor of *Lincoln Lore* inquired of the sculptor if there was a specific incident in Lincoln's life which he was attempting to portray. He replied it was but a sympathetic study of Lincoln as President.

Any student of Lincoln who has paid attention to Lincoln's changing features during his administration, will immediately identify this bronze study by Sculptor Keck as a portrait of the late 1863 period. In the preliminary model made by Mr. Keck, Lincoln is seated holding a manuscript in hand. In the final stage the manuscript was omitted for artistic symmetry.

There were two important events in Lincoln's life during the latter part of 1863 which were worthy of commemoration; the delivering of the Gettysburg Address and the issuing of the first annual national proclamation of Thanksgiving. The Gettysburg Address has been memorialized over and over again by heroic statues of Lincoln, and very naturally in every instance it has been a standing Lincoln who has been portrayed in the process of delivering the address.

We should expect to find a seated Lincoln as the author of the Thanksgiving Proclamation, and this heroic statue by Mr. Keck has that reverent repose and meditative mien that makes one feel as if the President is in communion with "the beneficent Father who dwelleth in the Heavens." A magnificent painting of Abraham Lincoln proclaiming Thanksgiving was recently completed by the famous American painter Dean Cornwell. Sculptor Keck and Artist Cornwell apparently have both been inspired by the same Lincoln—the President signing the Thanksgiving Proclamation.

When the late E. E. Whitney bequeathed to the town of Hingham, Massachusetts, an heroic bronze statue of Abraham Lincoln, something more than just another likeness of the President was created. It was a Lincoln who had come back to live among his kinsmen and to remind us all of that sacred institution which grew up with the nation.

It seems timely indeed that there should be dedicated, at the conclusion of seventy-five years of national Thanksgiving festivals, in the town of Lincoln's kinsmen, near The Old Ship Church, in the land of the Pilgrims, and in the fall of the year a Lincoln memorial to Thanksgiving.

march 1940

GOVERNOR TRUMBULL'S THANKSGIVING
PROCLAMATION 1780

PROCLAMATION

WHEREAS *it hath pleased Almighty GOD the Father of all Mercies, amidst the vicissitudes and calamities of War, to bestow Blessings on the People of these States...*

[body text illegible]

DONE *in Congress, this Eighteenth Day of October, 1780, and in the Fifth Year of the Independence of the United States of America.*

SAMUEL HUNTINGTON, *President.*

ATTEST.
CHARLES THOMSON, *Secretary.*

BY HIS EXCELLENCY

JONATHAN TRUMBULL, Esquire,

Governor, Captain-General, and Commander in Chief in and over the State of Connecticut, in America.

I HAVE thought fit, by and with the Advice of the Council, and at the Request of the House of Representatives, to approve and do hereby appoint THURSDAY the Seventh Day of December next, to be celebrated as a Day of public Thanksgiving and Prayer...

All servile Labour is forbidden on said Day.

GIVEN *under my Hand, in the Council Chamber at Hartford, the Seventh Day of November, 1780, in the Fifth Year of the Independence of the United States of America.*

JONATHAN TRUMBULL

THE CHICAGO AND EASTERN ILLINOIS RAILWAY MAGAZINE

Published Monthly in the Interest of All Employees of C&EI Railway and of Others Interested in Railroad Transportation and Its Development.

L. S. HOLMAN, Editor
Railroad Address—Freight Station, 317 East North Street, Danville, Illinois.
U. S. Mail Address—449 N. Jackson St., Danville, Illinois.
W. E. CALLENDER, Associate Editor, Chicago, Ill.
C. N. LAMMERS, Coal and Combustion Editor, Chicago, Ill.

Subscription—Complimentary to Employees.
Subscription—Complimentary to Contributors, Advertisers and Exchanges.
Subscription—General, $1.00 per year.

All employees are invited to contribute articles and news items of interest.

We especially solicit photographs for publication, and will return them upon request.

Thanksgiving

The coming of Thanksgiving season this year will be especially significant as it still finds us among the few nations with very much for which to be thankful. Our country, thanks to God, still gives to its inhabitants the right of freedom, free speech, and democratic form of government. When we sit at our tables the coming Thanksgiving day, we truthfully can give praise for the freedom fought for by the early pilgrims, which has extended down to the present day. The conflicts may have been many that we have endured as individuals as well as a nation during the past years of depression, it has meant deprivation for all alike and as we proudly sit today as Americans, believing we have been conquerors over every foe our hearts may be heavy over the fact that the millions out of employment are sharing only the bare necessities of life, but as our forefathers taught us so have we practiced the habit of sharing our good fortunes with those less fortunate and this Thanksgiving will give to each of us an opportunity not only to be thankful in a prayerful way but also in a material way.
—EDITOR

We present the following article written by Mr. Louis A. Warren entitled "Little Known Facts About Thanksgiving and Lincoln's Proclamation."

Colonial Thanksgiving Days

Governor William Bradford of the Massachusetts Colony was the founder of the Thanksgiving festival. As early as 1621 he called together the early settlers at Plymouth for the purpose of offering thanks to God for the preservation of their lives, food to sustain them, and clothing for their bodies. A man of strong religious convictions, Governor Bradford continued to call, periodically, seasons of thanksgiving. One of his earliest written manuscripts was entitled, "God's Merciful Dealings with us in the Wilderness." Abraham Lincoln's first American ancestor, Samuel Lincoln, had come to this very wilderness in 1637 and had settled not far from Plymouth. As a man of religious inclinations he undoubtedly participated in these early Thanksgiving festivals.

Occasional Thanksgiving Celebrations

During the Revolutionary War Congress recommended days of fasting and prayer at intervals throughout the long struggle. At its conclusion President Washington issued a proclamation naming Thursday, November 26, as a day for the citizens of the new nation to thank God for a constitutional form of government and the blessings which accompanied it.

It was not until 1815 that the festival was again revived on a national scale when President Madison urged the people to offer thanks on a day set apart by proclamation. It came at the close of the war with England and was a season of prayer and praise for national guidance and peace. For nearly half a century there were no more proclamations forthcoming, although governors of many states, at intervals, set apart certain days for the annual observance of the feast.

A Thanksgiving Advocate

The persistent effort of Sarah Josepha Hale, a New England woman, contributed much to the building of a favorable p u b l i c sentiment which eventually found expression in a national Thanksgiving Day observance. For twenty years Mrs. Hale labored diligently to emphasize the significance of a national fall festival. In a timely editorial prepared in 1852 she said: "Thanksgiving Day is the national pledge of Christian faith in God acknowledging him as the dispenser of blessings . . . . The observance of the day has been gradually extending, and for a few years past efforts have been made to have a fixed day which will be universally observed throughout the country . . . . The last Thursday in November was selected as the day, on a whole, most appropri-ate." Ten years later, in 1862, she was still pleading for the national feast day which, the preceding year, had been celebrated in twenty-four states and three territories. Although she had approached former Presidents with respect to setting aside a national holiday for praise and prayer, it was not until she appealed to Mr. Lincoln in 1863 that she found a sympathetic hearing.

The Preliminary Proclamations of Thanksgiving

Lincoln issued his first Presidential proclamation for a day of "public prayer, humiliation, and fasting" to be observed in September 1861. The following year a Sunday in April was set apart invoking divine guidance to "hasten the establishment of fraternal relations among all the countries of the world." It was in 1863, however, that two national fast days were proclaimed which paved the way for the establishment of the Thanksgiving festival as it is now observed.

A special day of prayer was proclaimed for Thursday, April 30, looking to "the pardon of our national sins and the restoration of our now divided and suffering country to its former and happy condition of unity and peace." Another day, Thursday, August 6, was set apart in which the people were requested to offer thanks for the Gettysburg victory and to call upon God "to subdue the anger which has produced and so long sustained a needless and cruel rebellion."

It was during this Thanksgiving season for Gettysburg and its victory that Mrs. Hale called to President Lincoln's attention the need of a Thanksgiving festival to be observed annually on an established day of the year. Lincoln complied with this request by issuing on October 3, 1863, the proclamation n a m i n g the last Thursday in November, 1863, as the first annual national Thanksgiving Day.

President Abraham Lincoln's Proclamation of Thanksgiving Issued October 3, 1863

The year that is drawing toward its close has been filled with the blessings of fruitful fields and healthful skies. To these bounties, which are so constantly enjoyed that we are prone to forget the source from which they come, others have been added, which are of so extraordinary a nature that they cannot fail to penetrate and soften the heart which is habitually insensible to the ever-watchful providence of almighty God.

In the midst of a civil war of unequalled magnitude a n d severity, which has sometimes seemed to foreign states to invite and provoke their aggressions, peace has been preserved with all nations, order has been maintained, the laws have been respected and obeyed, and harmony has prevailed everywhere, except in the theater of military conflict; while that theater has been greatly contracted by the advancing armies and navies of the Union.

Needful diversions of wealth and of strength from the fields of peaceful industry to the national defense have not arrested the plow, the shuttle, or the ship; the ax has enlarged the borders of our settlements, and the mines, as well of iron and coal as of the precious metals, have yielded even m o r e abundantly t h a n heretofore. Population has steadily increased, notwithstanding the waste that has been made in the camp, the siege, and the battlefield; and the country, rejoicing in the consciousness of augmented strength and vigor, is permitted to expect continuance of years with large increase of freedom.

No human counsel hath devised, nor hath any mortal hand worked out these great things. They are the gracious gifts of the Most High God, who, while dealing with us in anger for our sins, hath nevertheless remembered mercy.

It has seemed to me fit and proper that they should be solemnly, reverently, and gratefully acknowledged as with one heart and one voice by the whole American people. I do, therefore, invite my fellow-citizens in every part of the United States, and also those who are at sea and those who are sojourning in foreign lands, to set apart and observe the last Thursday of November next as a day of thanksgiving and praise to our beneficent Father who dwelleth in the heavens. And I recommend to them that, while offering up the ascriptions justly due to him for singular deliverances and blessings, they do also, with humble penitence for our national preverseness and disobedience, commend to his tender care all those who have become widows, orphans, mourners, or sufferers in the lamentable civil strife in which we are unavoidably engaged, and fervently implore the interposition of the almighty hand to heal the wounds of the nation, and to restore it, as soon as may be consistent with the Divine purposes, to the full enjoyment of peace, harmony, tranquility, and union.

In testimony whereof, I have hereunto set my hand, and caused the seal of the United States to be affixed.

Done at the city of Washington, this third day of October, in the year of our Lord one thousand eight hundred and sixty-three, and of the independence of the United States the eighty-eighth.

ABRAHAM LINCOLN

By the President:
William H. Seward,
Secretary of State.

Letter of Commendation
September 21, 1940

Mr. T. H. Kelch, General Agent
Chicago & Eastern Illinois Railroad
135 South LaSalle Street
Chicago, Illinois

Dear Mr. Kelch:

I wish to express my appreciation for the courteous and efficient service rendered me Sunday by Mr. E. H. Levis, one of your passenger traffic agents.

Unexpected news of serious illness in the family made it necessary for my wife to leave immediately for Montgomery, Alabama. Unfortunately, we received the news on Sunday and therefore were unable to secure from the bank cash for the rail ticket. Mr. Levis courteously explained the inability of the railroad to accept my personal check without references. I was able to supply satisfactory ones which he promptly checked, to protect your interest, and then arranged the transportation for us.

Mrs. Morthland and I frequently have travelled on your trains and always have been satisfied with the service. Mr. Levis, however, assisted us in a manner which we had no reason to expect. Consequently, I do wish to express my appreciation. His action has increased our good-will for your railroad.

Sincerely yours,

(Signed) Rex J. Morthland

I always sound my horn at railroad crossings. You never know what those crazy engineers will do next.

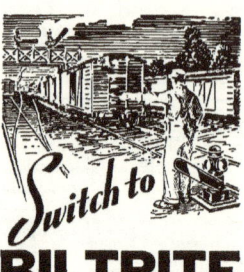

"CHRISTIAN RAILROAD" MAKES ITS LAST RUN

The Due West Railway, often called the nation's "most Christian Railroad" because its charter stated that no runs would be made on Sunday except in case of emergency, and no whiskey would be hauled, recently was abandoned by permission of the Interstate Commerce Commission.

The railway began operation in 1907. On one occasion, to rush a man to the hospital, it ran on Sunday. It never killed or injured anyone, never had an accident, never faced a law suit and never knowingly hauled liquor. Its engine once ran on New York's elevated.

The line is four miles long, from Due West to Donalds.

Editor's Note—This road did not collapse because it was called Christian, but it just goes to show that a Christian can be starved to death for lack of business.

A Proclamation
by
Anderson, Gov.

Foster, Document

128. OHIO. First National Thanksgiving proclamation after Civil War. Broadside, large 4to. "A Proclamation by Charles Anderson, Governor, THANKSGIVING Seventh day of December, 1865." AS NEW. Likely UNIQUE. 19.00.

In the preamble the Governor mentions that this is the first time that the state adopts as date the one set by the President of the U. S.

LINCOLN LORE

Bulletin of the Lincoln National Life Foundation - - - - - Dr. Louis A. Warren, Editor
Published each week by The Lincoln National Life Insurance Company, Fort Wayne, Indiana

Number 763	FORT WAYNE, INDIANA	November 22, 1943

"FIXINGS" FOR A HOOSIER THANKSGIVING

The approach of Thanksgiving day not only reminds one of the religious fervor of the Pilgrim fathers, but also calls attention to the festive side of pioneer life. The marvelous harvests which mother nature provided for her children of the plains and forests were phenomenal, indeed, when we observe that often no effort was put forth in the reaping, except the joy of gathering. These periods of bringing in nature's store was one of the bright spots on the frontier.

Recently there has been published under the title, *The Indiana Home*, a few notes on early pioneer life, which the late Logan Esarey, professor of History at Indiana University, used in his classroom over a period of many years.

A casual reading of Professor Esarey's notes, largely composed of family reminiscences, will allow one to orient the Lincolns in their early home in Indiana Territory. While this book contains but an occasional reference to the Lincolns, it does allow us to appreciate more fully the wonderful playground which surrounded Abraham Lincoln as a growing boy.

There are many testimonials in Esarey's book about the natural beauty of the southern Indiana country. He comments, "The region was perhaps as beautiful a forest as the world has ever known." His description of the trees and shrubbery is interesting, indeed. The story of the frontier, which brought so much pleasure to youth, is of timely interest at this season of the year, and it appears as if there were plenty of "fixings" for a Hoosier Thanksgiving in Lincoln's day.

Candy Bars for the Whole Year

The pioneer's harvests, contributed freely and with great abundance by mother nature, began in the early spring when the sap began to run. The gathering at the sugar camp was a social event of supreme importance to all, and offered about the only opportunity during the year for the younger element to sit up all night. The fire under the giant kettle had to be kept burning steadily; however, there were plenty of volunteers to watch the fire. Here the stock of candy for the year in the form of sugar hearts, diamonds, or little scalloped pies were stored in great jars at no cost except the fun of boiling down the sap.

"Pop" Made at Home

The sassafras shrub was one of the children's favorite bushes, and in the spring of the year its roots were dug up and the sassafras tea made from them was a drink not to be despised, either as a beverage or a spring tonic. The bark and root of the sassafras tree through the year was always within reach of the children of the forest.

Berries for Every Taste

Not even the children of today with all of their imported fruits have the variety of berries which the pioneer children harvested as their taste prompted. First came the June berry, and shortly after the mulberry, and also the wild strawberries which were so plentiful in some places that an early traveler stated that in riding through some localities "his horses hoofs were red with their juice." The large black dewberry also grew in great abundance and was equally enjoyed. For both stimulant and medicine the blackberry was a more welcome gift of nature, but not so tasty as the red raspberry which was not only harvested for immediate consumption, but with its cousin the blackberry, found its way into cordials.

The Pioneer's Fruit Basket

It was in the Fall of the year, more often associated with harvests, that nature made her best gifts to the pioneers. It seems as if the fun of gathering harvests, especially fruits and nuts, must have been of innate origin, certainly it was not work to the average pioneer boy. The pawpaw and the persimmons, which are unknown to most American boys and girls, were abundant in southern Indiana. Some of the finest persimmons the editor of *Lincoln Lore* ever ate were shaken one frosty morning from a persimmon tree which stood within a hundred feet of where Abraham Lincoln lived from the time he was seven until he was twenty-one.

The wild grape crop in the Indiana territory was abundant and the clusters of two varieties, October and fox grapes, were gathered for jellies, beverages, etc. The fox grapes were often found hanging on the vines until Christmas time. Nature usually provided some low tree as a grape basket into which the pioneer child could reach and satisfy his appetite without price. Along with the grapes should be mentioned red and black haws, also the wild plum and the crab apple which were often made into marmalade or fruit butter.

A Mixed Nuts Bowl

Possibly it was the gathering of the nut crop which offered, the boys especially, as much real fun as the harvesting of any other crop which nature provided, all un-aided. The shell or shag bark was the favorite nut tree. The harvesting of the shell, hickory, pecan, walnut and hazelnuts, according to Esarey, along with "the mellow autumn weather, the gorgeous decoration of the trees. . . . all combined to make this a carnival of nature for the country children."

Turkey in the "Raw"

The store of fruits from the forest and field were not so important to the pioneer as the store of game which was almost as easily obtained. Every Lincoln student is familiar with the story about the boy's first memorable experience in Indiana, told in these words: "A few days before the completion of his eighth year, in the absence of his father, a flock of wild turkeys approached the new log cabin and Abraham with rifle gun, standing inside, shot through a crack and killed one of them. Wild turkeys in the "raw," right in one's doorway.

Turkeys, although plentiful, did not appear in such vast numbers as wild pigeons which Audubon claimed, while they were in passage, entirely obscuring the sun. Quail were usually trapped at will and the pioneer table did not lack the usual tasty water fowl which were abundant along the rivers at certain seasons.

Small Game Everywhere

The woods and fields of southern Indiana were full of squirrels and rabbits and while the men of the pioneer days did not pay much attention to them, they were the practice pieces for the boys who were growing up, and they contributed much to the table. No squirrels or rabbits ever tasted so sweet as did those that the boy brought down with his own gun, or caught in his own trap.

The raccoon and other fur bearing animals of the smaller variety were abundant, and contributed much of interest to the ever changing pageantry of the wilderness.

Venison for All

The best gift nature had to offer the Indiana pioneer for both food and clothing was the deer. These animals were killed by the thousands and not only provided meat for the table through the year, but the hides were serviceable for gloves, shoes, pants, shirts, and suspenders. No animal outside the domesticated group ever contributed so much to the welfare of those living on the frontiers, the early hunters, and explorers, as did the deer.

It is not strange that one of Lincoln's friends who interviewed him with respect to his Indiana boyhood received this impression, "There was nothing sad nor pinched, and nothing of want, and no allusions to want, in any part of it. Lincoln's own description of his youth was that of a joyous, happy boyhood."

LINCOLN LORE

Bulletin of the Lincoln National Life Foundation - - - - - Dr. Louis A. Warren, Editor
Published each week by The Lincoln National Life Insurance Company, Fort Wayne, Indiana

MEDITATIONS FOR THANKSGIVING DAY

The forthcoming Thanksgiving Day may offer an appropriate environment for a few moments of meditation on the origin and subsequent history of this harvest anniversary abounding in holy and patriotic sentiments. Governor Bradford's proclamation to the Massachusetts Bay Colony "that all ye Pilgrims with ye wives and ye little ones do gather at ye meeting house on ye hill . . . to render thanksgiving to ye Almighty God for all his blessings" has set the pattern for more than three hundred and twenty-five years of subsequent proclamations pointing to the celebration of America's annual fall religious festival. This first proclamation expressed gratitude for "protection from the ravages of the savages" and freedom from "pestilence and disease" which had wrought such havoc during the first two years spent on the fringe of the bay. Later, other governors joined Bradford in setting apart annually by proclamation a day of Thanksgiving.

The scene changes to the Continental Congress of 1777 which set apart in December a day of prayer and praise "that under the providence of Almighty God these United States may receive the greatest of all blessings—independence and peace." Similar occasions were celebrated for six consecutive years, usually in December. The last resolution in 1783 expressed gratitude "that in the course of the present year hostilities have ceased, and we are left in the undisputed possession of liberty and independence." In 1887 another resolution spoke of "the ratification of the definite treaty of peace between the United States of America and his Britannic majesty." This paved the way for an instrument issued two years later which has been recognized as the first national Thanksgiving Proclamation issued by the President of the United States at the request of Congress.

The moving spirit in this national enterprise was Elias Boudinot, a descendant of a French Hugenot driven from Europe by religious persecution who presented a resolution in Congress on September 25, 1789, calling for "a joint committee of both Houses to be directed to wait upon the President of the United States to request that he would recommend to the people of the United States a day of public thanksgiving and prayer." This resolution embodied the idea that the nation should be thankful for "the opportunity peaceably to establish a constitution of government for their safety and happiness."

On October 3, 1789, President Washington complied with this resolution and issued a proclamation setting aside "Thursday the 26th day of November next" as the national Thanksgiving Day.

With the exception of a Thanksgiving Day proclaimed by Washington for the 19th of February, 1795, "for the seasonable control which has been given to a spirit of disorder in the suppression of the late insurrection (Whiskey Rebellion)" there was a lapse of presidential proclamations until the close of the War of 1812 when Madison set aside Thursday, April 3, 1815, as a day to thank God "for restoring to them the blessings of peace."

For nearly fifty years there were no more national Thanksgiving proclamations in America but the various states in the Union rallied to the call of the most enthusiastic exponent of the festival, Sarah Josepha Hale,

editor of *Godey's Lady Book* which magazine she utilized as a medium to publicize the festival. By the year 1856 she had been able to persuade governors of as many as twenty states to issue thanksgiving proclamations with the idea in view of nationalizing the festival.

Abraham Lincoln was the President whom Mrs. Hale encouraged to issue what has become known as the first annual Thanksgiving Proclamation. He was able to capture the New England spirit of devotion and patriotism which characterized the Pilgrim fathers and to preserve it for posterity by establishing a precedent for the annual observance of the day on the last Thursday of November.

That Lincoln was influenced by Washington's first proclamation is evident from the fact that he not only issued the document on Oct. 3, the same day utilized by Washington, but also set apart for the occasion "the last Thursday of November next" which also fell on the same day (Nov. 26) which Washington had selected.

With the exception of Andrew Johnson's choice in 1865 and U. S. Grant's designation in 1869, for a period of seventy-six years the last Thursday in November was proclaimed the national Thanksgiving day. The selection of this date had not been without careful consideration as its religious significance is familiar to those acquainted with the church calendar. The period preceding Easter known as Lent has its compliment in the preliminary period to Christmas known as Advent.

As early as the sixth century the first Sunday in Advent was established by its designation as the first Sunday following the "last Thursday in November." Inasmuch as the Friday and Saturday preceding Advent became days of fast and penance the preceding Thursday was the last day available for feasting. Hence the festal idea which was associated with the last Thursday in November.

It is not surprising that when President Franklin D. Roosevelt in both 1939 and 1940 changed the date of Thanksgiving from the last Thursday to the third Thursday, thereby destroying all the religious significance in the date, that Christian people remonstrated against it. Especially did they show their indignation when the President admitted that it had been done at the request of retail merchants who wanted a still longer pre-yule period in which to further commercialize the Christmas season which already is monopolized so greatly for mercenary ends.

Congressman Michener of Michigan offered a joint resolution in 1941 which would restore "the last Thursday in November as the annual Thanksgiving Day" and although it passed the House, the Senate amended it by striking out the word "last" and substituting the word "fourth" entirely ignoring the religious significance so clearly designated. Apparently the Senate, also was anxious to give the merchants a few more days to work on the public. The majority of last Thursdays will be fourth Thursdays. However, when the 29th or 30th of November falls on a Thursday, in celebrating the previous or fourth Thursday as Thanksgiving Day, we will be ignoring the religious significance of the approach to the Advent season.

COLONIAL GOVERNORS WHO MADE GOOD

By P. L. FRANKLIN

THE MONTH OF NOVEMBER, as we all know, brings us our national Thanksgiving holiday, and this red-letter day is associated in our minds with the Puritans of New England who established the custom of thanking the Almighty for blessings which would be regarded as short fare indeed by Americans of succeeding generations and more especially the present one.

Each Thanksgiving brings to mind the first two great governors of New England to whom goes the credit for a major part in establishing the first permanent colony in the northern portion of the United States. Needless to say, these two brave and pious men were John Carver and William Bradford, whose wise leadership went a long way toward establishing the Pilgrims in the New World along the desolate coast of Massachusetts.

The first governor of the Colony was John Carver who did not long survive his trip to the New World but who showed considerable ability, especially in his dealing with the savage tribes who inhabited the future state of Massachusetts.

Little is known of Governor Carver's early history. He was born in England about 1590 and his family were of the strict Puritan faith which was not at all popular in Great Britain at that time. Consequently Carver joined the Puritan colony at Leyden on the continent. He became known for his ability as a speaker and man of affairs and when the Puritans sojourning in Holland decided to move to the New World Carver was one of their representatives sent back to England to treat with the government for rights to establish a colony in America. The negotiations were successful and Carver and his partner in the deliberations were delegated to select a ship for the trip to the New World. The Mayflower was the result.

When the vessel arrived on the American coast it anchored temporarily at what is now Provincetown, and although the record is not clear, it is believed that at this point Carver was elected Governor for the next year.

The Pilgrims sailed on to what is now Plymouth and when the new civil year began on March 25, 1621, Carver had built for himself a good record as governor. He was re-elected for another year. He died suddenly in the latter part of April of the same year.

The first year of the Pilgrims in the New World was a trying one and called for all the ability which Governor Carver possessed to keep the colony afloat. His negotiations with the Indians were especially successful and set the stage for the friendly relations between white and red man which existed for the next few years, or until the colony was firmly on its feet.

To return to that first terrible winter, the records show that of the 102 brave people in the colony more than half were lost during that period. At one time there were only six or seven able-bodied persons in the colony, among them the doughty Captain Miles Standish and Elder Brewster, both of whom carried on with the ecourage of lions. They cared for the sick, buried the dead, and prepared what defense was needed against the Indians. When spring arrived came an experiment in communism which, like all others, were to follow, turned out to be a failure. Food was badly needed for the next winter. Crops were grown and put in a community warehouse, the work divided fairly among the men regardless of the size of their families. But those with little or no family objected to working as long as those with several mouths to feed, and Bradford, second great governor, and historian of the community wrote:

"This communitie was found to breed so much confusion & discontent, and retard much imployment that would have been to their benefite & comforte. For ye young men that were able and fitte for labour and service did repine that they should spend their time and strengthe to worke for other men's wives and children, without recompence. The strong had no more victails & cloaths then he that was weake & not able to doe a quarter ye other could, this was thought injustice".

Questions of age and rank also came up and caused dissension and the net result was that the first harvest was a great disappointment. So a private enterprise system was restored. Then Bradford wrote:

"So they begane to thinke that they might raise as much corne and obtain a beter crop than they had before done—that they might not still languish in miserie. At length, after much debate of things the Governor (with ye advice of ye chiefest amongst them) gave way that every man should sett corne for his owne perticular and in that regard trust to themselves * * * and so assigned to every family a parcell of land, according to the proportion of their number and to that

3

end ranged all boye and youthe under some familie."

The return to private enterprise, it is said, had immediate and astonishing results—all to the good. So much for one of the first comunistic experiments in America.

BUT TO RETURN to the political side: William Bradford was the second distinguished governor of the colony. More is known of his early life. He was born in Yorkshire, England, in March, 1588, was a landowner and a religious man, being seriously inclined from his childhood. He joined the church of Puritans established by William Brewster, who was to be one of his co-laborers in the Plymouth colony.

This act, however, only brought him into contempt with his neighbors, and the little band of Puritans was actually threatened with violence. So they pulled up stakes and emigrated to Holland. However, they still wanted to be Englishmen and in 1607 they drew up a contract with a Dutch captain to take them "across." The skipper, however, double-crossed them and betrayed them to the Dutch magistrates, sending some of them to prison and others back home. Bradford was one of those who got into jail. But he escaped after several months of confinement and went to Amsterdam where he went to work for a Frenchman. About the year 1609 he sold his land in England, but unfortunately lost it in a business venture. He then became active in the movement, frequently discussed, to form a Puritan colony in the New World. The company got a patent for land in Virginia—here they intended to locate—but a storm blew them out of their course and they landed in Plymouth harbor.

William Bradford

WHEN GOVERNOR CARVER DIED, Bradford, recognized as one of the ablest of the colonists, was elected governor in his place. And it proved to be a fortunate choice. Governor Bradford, by the way, favored a government of checks and balances and at his suggestion a council of five colonists was organized to restrict him. Later the number was increased to seven.

Realizing, as had Governor Carver before him, that the colony, if it were to survive, would have to remain on friendly terms with the Indians, one of his first acts as Chief Executive of the colony was to send a delegation to talk with Massasoit, the renowned chief of the redskins. As a result, a treaty of peace was made between the Indians and the colonists that lasted for some time.

When the food shortage became acute because of the communistic errors noted above, Governor Bradford sent a delegation to the Indians to get food to tide the colonists over the winter. He visited the natives himself, and as a result of his efforts the white men secured a supply ample enough to tide them over until the era of private enterprise and better times was ushered in. A conspiracy of Indians against the oppression of some white fur traders in what is now

Boston, was revealed to Governor Bradford by his Indian friend Massasoit. The colonists bought out the fur traders in an effort to promote peace and understanding with the aborigines.

King James of England had given to the so-called New England council a patent to land in that section, which included the territory occupied by the Plymouth colonists. Under Governor Bradford the settlers at Plymouth got from this council a patent to the tract including the colony of Plymouth. Then in 1634, with this added authority, Governor Bradford and his assistants were made into a judicial court. Six years later, at the request of the court, Governor Bradford conveyed to the colonies all his rights and titles except his fair proportion as a settler. This was done voluntarily and is a measure of the stature of the man.

The popularity of Governor Bradford grew steadily. His election as Governor was regularly assured. But for two terms he refused to stand as governor—a total of five years. Except for these two periods he held the office of Governor until his death which occurred May 9, 1657.

Governor Bradford was a family man and his domestic life was a happy one, despite the dangers and troubles of the times. He was first married in Holland to Dorothy May when he was 25 years of age. Like a good and faithful spouse she accompanied him on his adventures to the strange, new world, facing all the dangers and sufferings accompanying it. But Dorothy May came to an untimely end. While she was exploring in a small boat in and near Cape Cod harbor, the craft capsized and she was drowned. She was at the time searching for a place to establish a new settlement. This fatal accident occurred in December, 1620.

Three years later Governor Bradford was united in marriage with Alice Carpenter, widow of Edward Southworth. This lady was an English woman who came out to the colony to be married to the Governor whom she had known "back home" in his youth. He had five children in all—three sons and two daughters.

IN ADDITION TO BEING A DIPLOMAT, a statesman and adventurer, Governor Bradford was a man of letters, and one of considerable culture. He was educated in Latin and Greek and also knew something of the Hebrew language.

Governor Bradford's first literary effort—at least the first which has come down to us—is "A Diary of Occurrences." It covers the experiences of the colonists for the first thirteen months after they had landed at Plymouth, and it gives us a splendid idea of the first trials, the tribulations and the struggles of the Puritans in the wilds of Massachusetts. It was written in collaboration with Edward Winslow and was published in London in 1622. It immediately attracted wide attention all over England, and is now one of our most valued historical efforts on the colonies and was so popular at the time it appeared that it was republished in (See COLONIAL GOVERNORS, Page 32)

THANKSGIVING DAY dates from 1621. In that year, on a brisk November afternoon, winter on the wing, Governor Bradford of the Plymouth Colony offered praise to Almighty God and said a prayer in thanksgiving for the many blessings showered on the New World. This took place after the first harvest. After grace, dinner was served and a custom started.

Since then the feast of Thanksgiving has become outstanding. It is distinctly American, though now being observed by other nations, notably in South America. That, too, is as it should be since most of the foodstuffs served at a typical Thanksgiving Day dinner are native products of this continent—gifts to the world from South as well as North America.

Take the turkey, for instance—the center of attrac-

THANKSGIVING DINNER IN AMERICA

By JOHN JAY DALY

tion. Old Tom or young Moll offer the piece de resistance at any real Thanksgiving Day dinner. Their forebears crossed the border from Mexico, traveled north and were captured, cultivated and carved for the first settlers. These early Americans came near making the turkey America's national bird but the baldheaded eagle, after some debate, got the nod from the Pilgrim Fathers.

Although a native of Mexico, the turkey was actually domesticated in the United States. It crossed the Rio Grande primarily as a bird of fine feathers. The Mexicans never thought of eating it. They prized its glorious plumage over its meat. But the Pilgrim Fathers, glorifying the turkey on Thanksgiving Day, gave the bird a new role to play. They passed up the feathers for the drumsticks.

Nowadays, the turkey has reached commercial importance everywhere in the world. The history of this bird is written in native American lore, preserved in pottery design, emblazoned in legendary tales and its virtues extolled each year on the last Thursday in November.

Before the 18th century, the potato—another portion of Thanksgiving Day dinner—had never been grown norh of Colombia, South America. It next sprouted in the fields outside of Londonderry, New Hampshire, and was taken from there to Ireland in 1719, from whence it got its name—the Irish potato. It is also called the spud and even the scientists cannot explain that word in terms of etymology, but Irish tradition can—and Irish culture. This, too, in defiance of a belief that traces the spud's introduction into Ireland by Sir Walter Raleigh. He died a century before the spud was heard of in Ireland. On its arrival from the New World it was denounced so heavily by the leading pulpiteers and pamphleteers, both claiming it unfit for human consumption, that an organization was formed called The Society for the Prevention of Unclean Diet—and there, from the initial letters of these words, came the nickname, "spud".

The sweet potato, entirely different from the spud, is a member of the morning-glory family and supposedly another native of this continent. Christopher Columbus and his men "discovered" the sweet potato in the West Indies. But scientists tell us the Polynesians were enjoying sweet potatoes long before the year 100 A.D. Hawaii knew it in ancient times and it was under cultivation in New Zealand when that island was officially discovered. Incidentally, this species is considered by all experts as the true potato. The original potato, or the Irish potato, was called a ground nut by the native Colombians who claimed that the first man who ever saw one was Pedro de Ciera de Leon who lived in the Cauca Valley. When this potato was boiled it reminded the eaters of soaked chestnuts. Later, Spanish ships took the potato to Europe, carrying it to Ireland first. From there it went over to England where the English drummed up a mortal fear of it. Parliament even passed a law against the Irish potato and thus destroyed its market. This, along with the Society for the Prevention of Unclean Diet sent the potato back to America where it became known as strictly Irish. In truth, the Irish potato is not a potato at all, but a tuber. At least that's what experts say at the Department of Agriculture. The sweet potato, they will tell you, is the real article and a native American, too. Its boiled roots are not unlike chestnuts in flavor. Transplanted first to Spain and then to Portugal the sweet potato finally made its way back home and has been grown here ever since, throughout the hemisphere.

Corn, of course, is strictly an American dish. It was not even known in Europe, Asia or Africa, until after the discovery of America. The Indians developed corn from wild maize, the West Indian name for this product. It became popular from Canada to the Argentine where flint corn was first cultivated, making its way afterward to New England. Dent corn became the popular brand in the Middle West and popcorn an outgrowth of this. At the start, seventy different varieties of corn were grown, all from maize. The Aztecs brewed a beer they called Tizwen, using maize as the base. This was an alcoholic intoxicant made from fermented corn and later popularized by the Apaches. Afterwards it became known as the lager beer of Mexico. In some of our southern states cornlikker became another byproduct of maize. Even the corn husking bees of the Mid-West Corn Belt had their origin south of the Mexican border where maize or

Attending Thanksgiving Services in the Early Days

Masses—religious ceremonies—took place regularly at harvest time.

THE PUMPKIN, DECIDEDLY an American vegetable, and squash, along with many types of beans, were grown between rows of corn by the early Indians who made these delectable vegetables available in all parts of the Western Hemisphere. What they grew, in the beginning, was improved upon by the white man and still is being further refined. Out of the bean family, for instance, came the lima bean, the string bean, and the kidney bean, along with other types. Several kinds of squash are relished by the gourmets.

The tomato, native of South America and originally called the Love Apple, is also a worthy American contribution to the culinary art. From the good earth of western South America it raised its rosy cheeks first in the eleventh century. Though it looked pretty on the vine and gave grace to the garden the tomato, because of the passionate hue, perhaps, was ignored as food. The South Americans were just as afraid of the Love Apple as the English, later, feared the Irish potato. Anyway, the first three hundred years of the tomato's existence passed by the calendar before someone displayed enough nerve to eat one and learn what a delicious morsel was being by-passed. Then it ceased to be a garden ornament and became a necessity of life.

Even at that time, in the fourteenth century, the tomato was never taken straight. No one thought of extracting its juice as a breakfast beverage. No one stewed it, fried it, or even ate it raw. Instead, they pickled it. Then they made tomato preserves. At the moment, after six hundred years of intensive cultivation, it comes near being the queen of the table. Careful plant breeding has made it one of the most popular vegetables in America, more widely known here than in any other country.

AS FOR FRUITS AND NUTS, America has given a generous supply to the world. Some are distinctly native, others imported and further cultivated until their own home lands hardly recognize them. At first, the native stock grew wild and in such profusion that the Indians did not bother to cultivate many of the finest fruits and nuts.

Blueberries, first of the fruit family to gain notice here, were found on the shore of Lake Champlain as far back as 1615. In later years they were cultivated in the Far Western states. But they are still found wild in New England even on the islands of Martha's Vineyard and Nantucket. The red raspberry is also a contribution from North America—and it goes to the world along with the blackberry and the huckleberry, always grown luxuriously throughout the Southland. The blackberry and the strawberry, in their highest cultivated form, are strictly the gifts of Dixie. Strawberries and cream, somewhat akin to the nectar of the gods, make a tasteful dish for the breaking of the morning fast. Sauce made from cranberries, another American crop, tops the Thanksgiving Day meal. These berries grow larger here than anywhere else.

Breakfast, dinner and supper—lunch, too—all three meals could be made up from menus strictly American, from the juices that break the early morning fast—another innovation of the American diet—to the nuts that are passed around after the napkins are thrown carelessly across the tables and the chairs moved back, even to the cigars and cigarettes whose tobaccos are native grown. America's contribution to the dining table are exceedingly good to the palate.

THE PEANUT IS A NATIVE of Brazil. So, too, the Brazil nut, named in honor of that virtual empire, the United States of Brazil, the largest political division on the South American continent. The Brazil nut has many uses: first as a fatty food and then as a contributor of oil for lubrication purposes. Another native of Brazil is the cashew.

The pecan, one of the choice nuts, is a native of Texas, Louisiana and Mexico, and was first mentioned by De Soto. The pecan tree is one of the glories of the Great Southwest, especially in the Lone Star State.

In the United States, though, the peanut reigns supreme. It got its start down in Brazil, went to Africa and was brought to the United States by Negro slaves. Here it makes its home mostly in the ball parks and movie houses. A baseball fan without a bag of peanuts is like a baby without a rattle. Use of the peanut for roasting and eating is strictly American. Elsewhere these nuts are used for making oil and for feeding livestock. Lately, however, peanut oil, once solely an import, has come to be used on the American table, mainly in salads.

And tobacco. Sir Walter Raleigh, the Englishman, helped popularize this strictly American plant. Christopher Columbus, of course, was the first European to see tobacco grown. He came across the weed in the West Indies where the natives were fond of it. They made the first cigars. In the United States, even before colonial days, Indians smoked, chewed and even drank tobacco. Originally a tropical plant, it was used by young and old, men and women, and considered good for health. It had, the Indians believed, great medical value.

UNDOUBTEDLY, THE INDIANS were the first to use tobacco and many a pipe of peace was filled with its aromatic substance, but the weed had traveled a great deal since, now going around the world. There are more kinds of tobacco now than there are women's styles, but the choice tobaccos of our Southern States and the rare, broad leafed tobacco of the North, grown under cover, still lead the world's trade. American tobacco has no equal. That is why a good meal is usually topped off with a smoke—cigarettes for the ladies, cigars for the men.

From the time a man sits down to a sumptuous dinner, say on Thanksgiving Day, beginning with an appetizer and ending with a Havana cigar, his menu can be largely native American, even though typographically it be set in purest French.

By the same virtue, when a man comes down to breakfast in the morning and has placed before him some of the rare juices raised in this country he enjoys a privilege known in few other nations on earth.

After making a lecture tour of the United States not long ago, an English writer in a farewell radio speech, just before his departure for home, said:

"What I shall miss most about America are its juices—the like of which you'll find nowhere else on earth—tomato juice, (See THANKSGIVING, Page 32)

BRAZIL

(Continued from Page 16)

the emergency, the Army set a junta which laid plans for the elections. In this contest, the first of its kind since 1930, Eurico Gaspar Dutra, the government-backed candidate was an easy winner. In the background was the shadow of Getulio Vargas who had quietly arranged for considerable support for Dutra, who had been his Minister of War.

The elevation of General Dutra to the Presidency of Brazil was the fruit of historical circumstances. He was not a politician in the true sense of the word, and by nature is an honest, and competent military man. In assuming the Presidential chair in 1946 President Dutra kept a keen eye on the activities of the Communists, since the previous arrangement of Vargas and the Reds had never appealed to him, and word got out that the friends of the Kremlin were overdue for a separation process.

Once out of prison Prestes moved with phenomenal speed, and within a few months was holding a seat in the Brazilian Senate, where he proceeded at once to work feverishly for the welfare of Moscow. Neither did he lose any time inviting hot water. His bold and arrogant activity provoked limited military restrictions against the Party, and Moscow, apparently concerned, hurriedly sent in a crack trouble-shooter, Ambassador Jacob Suritz, a bosom friend of the late Ambassador Oumansky and well versed on the Red network in Latin America.

In a matter of hours after his arrival, Ambassador Suritz went into a huddle with Prestes and other Red leaders in Rio. It was believed that Suritz "suggested" a change of tactics, and more important, a change of pace. Prestes slowed down his delivery and prolonged for nearly a year any punitive action against the Party in Brazil. Moscow had evidently given Suritz a free hand for harmonizing the Network in the entire Southern Hemisphere, holding him responsible for the success or failure of his assignment.

Suritz often sought the counsel of Andri Gromyko, Soviet Ambassador to Washington, who also nailed down the Red transmission center in Cuba, leaving a Charge de' Affairs in Havana for necessary desk-cleaning. Cuba, like Brazil was tolerating a Communist Party membership of nearly 200,000 and making it necessary for Gromyko and Suritz to occasionally compare notes on how the other was doing. The transmission center, for years located in Mexico City was transferred to Cuba, after Oumansky had knocked at the gates of eternity, and highly confidential matter, previously sent by agent and couriers from the Mexican capital was now routed to Brazil via Cuba, where some of the "best" brains of the Communist Party had established residence.

By virtue of a day-to-day report, made possible by an uninterrupted courier service, Prestes was able to maintain close contact with top-flight Reds in Moscow, Cuba and other Red cells in Latin America. This assembly-line cell and spy system must still be recognized as a terrible menace to the defense and security of the Western Hemisphere.

As the calendar of 1947 rolled around, President Dutra was having election embarrassment in the state of Sao Paulo, where a Communist-Progressive-supported candidate, a disciple of Vargas had just walked into the office as Governor. Barros was not considered a Communist and merely used them in a political maneuver. Dutra, who had opposed Barros, swallowed hard, but ordered his War Minister General DaCosta to guarantee the inauguration of the victor.

This defeat for Dutra stimulated a retaliatory move and he ordered a slight curb on all Communist activities. Prestes, always in step from sun-up to sun-up or twenty-four hours a day, made application to register the Communist Party of Brazil as a political organization. The Superior Electoral Tribunal denied this request with the words: "The Communist Party of Brazil is not an organization of national and patriotic aims, but rather some sort of a Russian scheme worked under the domination of the Third International."

The handwriting was on the wall, and in 1948 Brazil ruptured relations with Soviet Russia; bounced Prestes out of the Senate, and outlawed the Communist Party, driving it underground. But that was yesterday.

Today, the Brazilian Reds, still well organized, function almost entirely underground. Prestes is in hiding, still working night and day for Moscow . . . and still a very dangerous man. Today, Dr. Getulio Vargas has become a very, very important man in the Western Hemisphere. And tomorrow, events commanding special international interests will be recorded in paradoxial and fascinating Brazil, the place where anything can happen . . . and does.

HERESIES

(Continued from Page 22)

The Paulicians were an Evangelical Christian church that dated from the Fifth Century. According to the Chronicon, the Paulicians were Manicheans and were named after Paul of Samosata. They spread over Asia Minor and Armenia. Constantine of Mananali based his teachings on the Gospel and Epistles of Paul, but repudiated other scriptures. The movement spread to Bulgaria, Syria, and Palestine, where they were called Publicani. The Crusaders found them in many places. The Armenian Patriarch John IV (ca. 728) advised that Nerses, his predecessor, had chastised the sect, but ineffectually; that after his death (ca. 554) they had continued to lurk in Armenia. The 18th Century found them in their old haunts. Paulician doctrines may be enumerated

as follows: 1. They denied the Virgin birth of Jesus and allegorized Mary. 2. They assailed the Cross and held Jesus Christ was a cross: they smashed crosses where they could. 3. They repudiated Peter, did not accept his repentence and tears, and styled him a denier of Christ. 4. They allegorized the Eucharist and denied that bread and wine should be offered as a sacrifice. 5. They anathematized Mani but were dualists. 6. They accepted the Heavenly Father and an Evil Demiurge. 7. They held the monkish garb was revealed by Satan to Peter at the baptism. 8. They held the water in baptism was bath water. 9. They held that Jesus was an angel born of woman. Christ, they held was only a creature, but called Him Son.

(To Be Continued)

OUT-SELLING US ?

(Continued from Page 8)

in exchange. And yet Moscow accuses us of trying to gain economic domination and out-sells us in other countries on political issues.

Since the close of hostilities America has reduced her armed forces to a danger point—as we are learning to our sorrow in Korea today. During the same time Russia has engaged in building the mightiest military machine in history. And yet Moscow calls us "warmongers" while posing as the only true "champions of peace". Using every means at her command, even the United Nations, Moscow has been and continues to spread her propaganda far and wide—and apparently the lie continues to win over the truth.

As a result, we now find ourselves backed up against a stone wall. We are compelled to use armed force against the aggressors and to risk American lives. But there is a better way—and a cheaper way. If we can only sell our way of life to others—and why can't we?—then military force might be unnecessary. If we can win the hearts of other people, if we can properly inspire them with the love of freedom and peace and with a determination to reach for it—and what could be easier?—then infantry divisions and air groups and naval task forces would eventually become outmoded. It seems that schoolboys, given the tools we have, should be able to achieve this goal.

How long are we going to permit lies to triumph over truth? How long is it going to take us to learn to put our advertising skill and our selling know-how and our missionary zeal to the task of properly taking our message to the world? How long are we going to sit back and let Moscow Communists outsell us?

PRESIDENTS

(Continued from page 18)

stant dependence of man upon the divine favor for all the good gifts of life and

Contents of This Issue

Subscription price $2.00 a year.
Address, 511 Eleventh Street, N. W.,
Washington 4, D. C.

---

health, and peace and happiness so early
in our history made the habit of our
people, finds in the survey of the past
year new grounds for its joyful and grateful manifestation.

* * *

WILLIAM H. TAFT: At peace,
within and without, free from the per-
turbations and calamities that have afflicted other peoples, rich in harvests so
abundant and in industries so productive
that the overflow of our prosperity has
advantaged the whole world, strong in the
steadfast conservation of the heritage of
self-government bequeathed to us by the
wisdom of our fathers and firm in the
resolve to transmit that heritage unim-
pared, but rather improved by good use,
to our children and our children's children
for all time to come, the people of this
country have abounding cause for con-
tented gratitude.

* * *

WOODROW WILSON: "Righteous-
exalteth a nation" and "peace on earth,
good will toward men" furnish the only
foundations upon which can be built the
lasting achievements of the human spirit.

The year has brought us the satisfaction
of work well done and fresh visions of
our duty which will make the work of the
future better still.

* * *

CALVIN COOLIDGE: We shall do
well to accept all favors and bounties
with a becoming humility, and dedicate
them to the service of the righteous cause
of the Giver of all good and perfect gifts.
As the nation has prospered let all the
people show that they are worthy to pros-
per by rededicating America to the service of God and man.

'DAVID'

(Continued from Page 17)

The third, or small David, called the
David-Appollo, of the Bargello, is the one
which found its way to our National Gal-
lery and is the one in which it is said we
can best believe as depicting the shep-
herd lad of the Bible. While it is not
known just when he began this work, it is
believed that Michelangelo did the statue
while engaged in the work on the Sacristy
of San Lorenzo. It is generally considered
to be the more gracefully posed figure of
the two Davids. At once we are impressed with the smallness of the figure
while the features are pleasing to the
imagination. We find a striking contrast
in the early colossal figure and this small
David of a quarter of a century later.
The subtlety of expression, the slow,
graceful movement of the pose, represent
the stage of development in the interval
separating the two marbles. It represents
the last of the great line of Renaissance
Davids.

THANKSGIVING

(Continued from Page 6)

orange juice, grapefruit juice, papaya juice,
all the juices . . . "
He sighed, and a sob shook his voice as
he sang a paen in honor of the foodstuffs
which America—in fact, all the Americans
—gave to the world.
The best example, of course, is that
Thanksgiving Day dinner that has become
so famous, Thanksgiving Day being the
most typical as well as the oldest of all
American holidays and therefore deserving
of special respect. It has been our greatest feast since the days of the Pilgrims
though it was not proclaimed a national
holiday until after the Revolutionary
War. Then, George Washington set aside
the first national Thanksgiving Day—November 26, 1789. Strange to say, since
then it has been celebrated in different
months, even in March, April and May.
Not until 320 years after the first celebration staged by the Pilgrims did Thanksgiving Day become a legal holiday—and
that was in 1941. Then, and not till then,
was it acclaimed by Congressional action:
the outstanding holiday that Americans,
like us, like to celebrate.

COLONIAL GOVERNORS

(Continued from Page 4)

abbreviated form in Purchas' Pilgrims,
three years after it first appeared in print.
The remarks of Governor Bradford, so
painstakingly set down, were drawn on by
Nathaniel Morton, Governor Hutchinson
and other historians in their treatises on
the Massachusetts colonies.
Governor Bradford, during his active
life in the colonies, spent a great deal of
time in writing, but few of his words were
published until after his death—perhaps
because only then did the people begin to
realize the bigness of the man.
Among his literary productions were
"Some Observations of God's Merciful
Dealings with Us in this Wilderness"; "A
Word to Plymouth"; "A Word to New
England"; "Diary of Occurrences"; "Me-
moir of Elder Brewster"; "History of the
Plymouth Plantation," and many others.
Some of Bradford's works were fragmen-
tary and most of them, including the above
were reprinted in Alexander Young's
"Chronicles of the Pilgrim Fathers." They
are invaluable in giving us a background
of life in the New England colonies.
So much for the first two really great
Governors in American history, men who
did so much to help lay the foundations
for our nation.

EMPIRE

(Continued from Page 2)

in that direction as contained in the
Charter. It has refused to take part in
all specialized agencies of the United Nations which seek to improve human life
and secure freedom to man.
Present world unrest results from the
futile attempt of free countries to co-
operate with the slave empire called the
Soviet Union. That empire is a throw-
back to the Dark Ages. It is the enemy
of human liberty. It carries within itself the seeds of death, and will go down
as all slave empires have gone down. But
free nations everywhere can help to shield
the world from this Mongol curse by re-
forming the United Nations into a really
free system, ready to strike down this
latest foe of mankind.

STATEMENT OF OWNERSHIP, MANAGEMENT,
CIRCULATION, ETC., REQUIRED BY ACT
OF CONGRESS, AUGUST 24, 1912, OF THE
NATIONAL REPUBLIC.
Published monthly at Washington, D. C., for
November 1, 1950.
Publisher: The National Republic Publishing Co.,
Muncle, Ind., and Washington, D. C.
Editor: Frank P. Litschert, Muncle, Ind., and
Washington, D. C.
Managing Editor: Walter S. Steele, Bethesda, Md.
Business Manager: Walter S. Steele, Bethesda, Md.,
and Muncle, Ind.
Owners: Frank P. Litschert, Washington, D. C.;
Walter S. Steele, Bethesda, Md.
Known bondholders, mortgagees and other security
holders owning or holding one per cent or more of total
amount of bonds, mortgages or other securities: none.
WALTER S. STEELE.
Sworn to and subscribed before me this 12th day
of September, 1950.
FRANK X. GROSS, Notary Public.
(My commission expires February 28, 1951)

Lincoln Proclamation Made Thanksgi

Journal Capital 25 1950

(Last in a series of articles on the history of Thanksgiving.)

By RALPH AND ADELIN LINTON

By 1880 the Thanksgiving feast had become a strong American tradition.

Pioneers, seeking new homes in frontier territories, carried the tradition with them and continued to give thanks for the bounty of God in the familiar way.

But the pioneers wanted to feel that they were sharing this occasion with the folks back home, saying the same prayers on the same day, gorging on the same foods at the same time.

Sentiment was continually growing stronger toward making Thanksgiving an annual holiday in which Americans of all faiths and backgrounds could join in offering thanks to the Creator for their homes in this free and bounteous land.

The most untiring worker toward this goal was Mrs. Sara Josepha Hale, the famous editor of Godey's Lady's Book of Philadelphia.

For almost forty years she conducted a campaign to make Thanksgiving a national holiday. It is highly probable that she even paid a personal visit to Abraham Lincoln to put her case before him.

In any event, on October 3, 1863, in the midst of the Civil War, Lincoln issued a National Thanksgiving Proclamation, the first since that of Washington in 1789.

Fixed Date For 80 Years

The Lincoln proclamation, which fixed an official Thanksgiving date for 80-odd years, follows:

"The year that is drawing toward its close has been filled with the blessings of fruitful fields and healthful skies.

"To these bounties, which are so constantly enjoyed that we are prone to forget the source from which they come, others have been added, which are of so extraordinary a nature that they cannot fail to penetrate and soften the heart which is habitually insensible to the ever-watchful providence of Almighty God.

"In the midst of a civil war of unequaled magnitude and severity, which has sometimes seemed to foreign states to invite and provoke their aggressions, peace has been preserved with all nations, order has been maintained, the laws have been respected and obeyed, and harmony has prevailed everywhere, except in the theater of military conflict; while that theater has been greatly contracted by the advancing armies and navies of the Union.

"Needful diversions of wealth and strength from the fields of peaceful industry to the national defense have not arrested the plow, the shuttle, or the ship; the ax has enlarged the borders of our settlements, and the mines, as well of iron and coal as of the precious metals, have yielded even more abundantly than heretofore.

'No Human Counsel'

"Population has steadily increased, notwithstanding the waste that has been made in the camp, the siege, and the battlefield, and the country, rejoicing in the consciousness of augmented strength and vigor, is permitted to expect continuance for years with large increase of freedom.

"No human counsel hath devised, nor hath any mortal hand worked out these great things. They are the gracious gifts of the most high God, who, while dealing with us in anger for our sins, hath nevertheless remembered mercy.

"It has seemed to me fit and proper that they should be solemnly, reverently, and gratefully acknowledged as with one heart and one voice by the whole American people.

"I do, therefore, invite my fellow-citizens in every part of the United States, and also those who are at sea and those who are sojourning in foreign lands, to set apart and observe the last Thursday of November next as a day of thanksgiving and praise to our beneficient Father who dwelleth in the heavens.

"And I recommend to them that, while offering up the ascriptions justly due to him for such singular deliverances and blessings, they do also, with humble penitence for our national perverseness and disobedience, commend to his tender care all those who have become widows, orphans mourners, or sufferers in the lamentable civil strife in which we are unavoidably engaged, and fervently implore the interposition of the almighty hand to heal the wounds of the nation, and to restore it, as soon as may be consistent with the Divine purposes, to the full enjoyment of peace, harmony, tranquillity, and union."

Roosevelt Breaks Precedent

With the Lincoln Proclamation Thanksgiving became a legal holi-

ving Legal Holiday

day on which the whole Nation closes its shops, offices, schools, and banks, and offers its thanks to the Deity for the blessings of this free and bountiful land.

Although, officially, the date is set each year by presidential proclamation, the fourth Thursday of November became the traditional Thanksgiving Day.

Great was the consternation, therefore, when in 1939, Franklin Delano Roosevelt, that famous breaker of precedents, proclaimed November 23rd, the third Thursday, as Thanksgiving.

The reason for the change was that the merchants had complained that the interval between Thanksgiving and Christmas was so short that they could not make proper provision for the December holiday rush.

Although this seemed a sensible adjustment, there were loud protesting outcries in the land.

Irate Republicans appealed to the Pilgrim Fathers, the Founding Fathers, and even the Constitution.

Football coaches, whose schedules for the all-important Thanksgiving Day games had been arranged on the assumption that Nov. 30 was the day, groaned and cursed That Man in the White House.

Country Divided

The country was divided into two camps: those who accepted the proclamation and feasted on the 23rd, and those who held to the traditions of their forefathers and dined on the 30th.

Harassed mothers didn't know when to cook the turkey, for some of the children in school had their holiday on the 23rd and some on the 30th.

After two years of this confusion, Thanksgiving went back to the fourth Thursday. It is doubtful that any future President will flaunt tradition again by changing the date.

We have come a long way from the Eleusinian Mysteries of the ancient Greeks to the eccentricities of the New Deal. But this wide span merely goes to show that human nature has not changed greatly over the centuries.

The emotional need to express gratitude to the Deity for the bounty of the earth is ages old, as is likewise the joy of human beings in coming together for feasting and sharing this bounty with those they hold dear.

End Of Series

LINCOLN LORE

Bulletin of the Lincoln National Life Foundation · · · · · · Dr. Louis A. Warren, Editor
Published each week by The Lincoln National Life Insurance Company, Fort Wayne, Indiana

Number 1181   FORT WAYNE, INDIANA   November 26, 1951

LINCOLN'S LAST THANKSGIVING DINNER

Friends of Abraham Lincoln expressed their admiration for him in the fall of 1864 by making sure that his table would be well provided with delicacies on Thanksgiving Day. The fact that the noon day meal served on Thursday, November 24th at the White House proved to be the President's last Thanksgiving dinner, contributes something to the human interest element in the story. The Lincoln Papers in the Library of Congress reveal that from far and near parcels of food both in large and small quantities reached the executive mansion for the gala occasion, or at least sometime during the season of festivities.

Of course the most important Thanksgiving donation from the viewpoint of the youngest boy Tad, at least, was a pair of turkeys, making four drumsticks on which he could work. These turkeys were presented by Walter C. Simmons of Providence, R. I. and he advised Mr. Lincoln that they had been sent on November 21. Mr. Simmons wrote in part: "I have today taken the liberty of forwarding to you by Adams Express two Rhode Island turkeys for your Thanksgiving dinner. They are Narragansett turkeys celebrated in New England and New York markets as being the best in the world."

Apparently these live turkeys did not arrive in time for Tad to form an attachment for them as on a previous Thanksgiving occasion when he refused to have a turkey killed because it had become "a good turkey" and followed him about the White House lawn. The episode ended by the President signing a reprieve for Tom Turkey. The paper was immediately presented by Tad to the executioner and the turkey's life saved for the time being at least.

On the same day the turkeys were forwarded George B. Smith of Troy, New York sent a piece of beef, in case there were guests who did not prefer turkey. This is the note which accompanied the presentation: "I ask you to accept from me the enclosed, a choice piece of roasting beef as a small token of respect for you, not only as the chief executive but as a man, which I hope you will receive in time for Thanksgiving dinner." The day after the beef arrived Lincoln received notice from Carlos Pierce of the National Sanitary Fair at Boston that the sale of the mammoth ox "Gen. Grant" had realized over $3,300." The President had been informed a few days before that through some voting contest at the fair the ox had been awarded to him and he immediately donated it to the fair. He must have been thankful indeed that so much money could be realized for so worthy a project. Possibly he felt the roast beef on that Thanksgiving Day, at least, was more symbolical for gratitude than the turkeys.

One of the earliest harvest gifts which may well have lasted over the Thanksgiving period, if not eaten by members of the President's cabinet, was a box of apples. They were presented by E. Bently of Tioga, Penn. and probably reached the White House about the first week in November, just before election. In fact the apples had a political flavor as indicated by the letter written by Mr. Bently. He said: "This day (Oct. 31) I have sent you by express a small box of apples. . . . The apples on top are just put in to fill up, they are fall Seek-no-further, and Lyman's Pumpkin Sweet. The green ones in one end are McClellan apples two faced and really good for nothing only show. The remainder of the box are a new variety and for want of a better name we call them 'Lincoln apples.' They are good looking, good to keep, good to eat, and very prolific. They are A. No. 1.

"Now if you are not exactly satisfied with the name you may call a cabinet council and lay the matter and the apples before them and if you and they can agree upon a better name they shall hereafter be called by it."

Previous to the gift of apples came a fruit cake presented by Mrs. Harkinson of Philadelphia who had five sons in the service. If this cake was allowed to age over a considerable period it may have graced the table. Possibly this gift may have been recalled when the President three days before Thanksgiving Day wrote the famous letter to the widow Bixby whom he had been informed had lost five sons in the service and which letter along with provisions was presented to the widow on Thanksgiving Day at Boston.

Certainly a Thanksgiving dinner in the South, and the city of Washington in that day at least was a southern city, would not be complete without sweet potatoes. The potatoes for Lincoln's table, however, came from Gloucester City, New Jersey, a whole barrel of them. They were sent by Alexander E. Powell on November 12 and were valued on the express bill of lading at $5.00, the express charges prepaid were $2.25.

For dessert on Thanksgiving to accompany the fruit cake there may have been some tasty dish made from canned peaches as the Lincolns received a whole case of them from H. C. Peters of York Springs, Pa. on November 21. We may feel certain nothing was lacking in the way of delicacies to make this feast a memorable one.

Some other items of food were started on their way before Thanksgiving but could not have reached the table of the Lincoln's until after the festivities were over. R. C. Small representing the Sanitary Fair at San Francisco on Nov. 22 sent the President a sample of a gigantic cheese "which weighed some 4000 pounds."

The President had at least two visitors on Thanksgiving Day, who had apparently chosen the occasion as an opportunity to approach him when possibly he might be influenced by the religious atmosphere of the day. Something caused the President to write out a memorandum dated Dec. 3, 1864 with respect to his visitors. He noted: "On Thursday of last week two ladies from Tennessee came before the President, asking the release of their husbands held as prisoners of war at Johnson's Island . . . one of the ladies urged that her husband was a religious man, . . . the President ordered the release of the prisoners, when he said to this lady: 'You say your husband is a religious man; tell him when you meet him, that I say I am not much of a judge of religion, but that, in my opinion, the religion that sets men to rebel and fight against their government, because, as they think, that government does not sufficiently help some men to eat their bread in the sweat of other men's faces, is not the sort of religion upon which people can get to heaven.'" The memorandum was signed by the President.

Harper's Weekly forwarded 200,000 copies of their Thanksgiving issue to the boys in the field. It presented a two page drawing by Thomas Nast featuring the Thanksgiving festival. Aside from his own family observation of Thanksgiving Day, Lincoln must have received great satisfaction in knowing that "his boys" in the larger family circle, in which he was known as Father Abraham, were also enjoying the fruits of an abundant harvest.

LINCOLN LORE

Bulletin of the Lincoln National Foundation - - - - - Dr. Louis A. Warren, Editor
Published each week by The Lincoln National Life Insurance Company, Fort Wayne, Indiana

Number 1233 FORT WAYNE, INDIANA November 24, 1952

LINCOLN'S ATTRIBUTE OF THANKFULNESS

One of the characteristics which Abraham Lincoln revealed in both his writings and behavior was the attribute of thankfulness. His discerning parents must have cultivated this desirable quality when he was but a child. There is evidence that each day Thomas Lincoln, the father, paused before their frugal meals to thank God for such blessings as were provided. There has come down from Dennis Hanks, a member of the household, a tradition that on one occasion, when the food on the table was limited to potatoes, Abe commented after the usual grace had been pronounced, "I call them mighty poor blessings."

A copy of the *Uncollected Letters of Abraham Lincoln* by Gilbert A. Tracy in the Foundation Library bears the signature of Theodore Roosevelt. Several passages in the book are pencil marked presumably by him. One of his delineations is this paragraph in a letter written by Lincoln in 1857 to Hannah Armstrong in her troubled situation:

"Gratitude for your long-continued kindness to me in adverse circumstances prompts me to offer my humble services gratuitously. . . . It will afford me an opportunity to requite, in a small degree, the favors I received at your hand, and that of your lamented husband when your roof afforded me a grateful shelter, without money and without price."

The most enduring memorial to Lincoln's spirit of gratefulness is his Proclamation of Thanksgiving issued on Oct. 3, 1863, setting apart, on the last Thursday of November in that year, what proved to be America's first annual national Thanksgiving festival. After enumerating the many "gracious gifts of the most high God" the President continued, "It has seemed to me fit and proper that they should be solemnly, reverently and gratefully acknowledged."

About a month before Lincoln issued his proclamation he wrote a letter to

James C. Conkling in which he expressed appreciation for those who "lent a hand" in the progress of the Union cause: He mentioned, "The great northwest. . . New England, Empire, Keystone and Jersey . . . the Sunny South too . . ." and continued, "The job was a great national one and let none be banned who bore an honorable part in it." Lincoln then concluded the paragraph with this expression of appreciation: "Thanks to all. For the great republic—for the principle it lives by, and keeps alive—for man's vast future—thanks to all."

The issuing of the proclamation of the following year, 1864, called for the obseravnce of the last Thursday in November as Thanksgiving Day and its reoccurrence assured the annual aspect of the festival. The President signed this proclamation on October 20 and two days later, while still in the spirit of the message

---

Thanks to all. For the great republic—for the principle it lives by, and keeps alive—for man's vast future—thanks to all.

---

calling for the giving of thanks, wrote a letter to General Sheridan overflowing with gratitude. The general by a decisive victory on Oct. 19 had brought the Shenandoah Valley campaign to a close and the President acknowledged his appreciation in these words:

"With great pleasure I tender to you and your brave army the thanks of the nation, and my own personal admiration and gratitude."

But the Thanksgiving season of 1864, the last festival of this kind that Lincoln was to enjoy, created an atmosphere which was to produce a far more famous writing. On November 21 he wrote his remarkable letter to the widow, Lydia Bixby of

Boston, whom Lincoln had been advised had lost five sons in the war. The letter was delivered to her personally by Adjutant-General Schouler, the morning following Thanksgiving Day.

So much controversy has developed about various facets associated with the episode, that attention has been diverted until the casual reader and the Lincoln student as well may have failed to appreciate the real gem of English literature. We might think of the letter as the finest illustration extant of Abraham Lincoln's attribute of thankfulness. Penned as it was almost on the eve of Thanksgiving Day, it is not strange that the religious fervor of the season should find expression in Lincoln's petition to God for the sorrowful widow. It was the President's prayer "that Our Heavenly Father assuage the anguish of your bereavement, and leave you only the cherished memory of the loved and lost, and the solemn pride that must be yours to have laid so costly a sacrifice on the altar of freedom."

Yet Lincoln contemplated: "How weak and fruitless must be any word of mine which should attempt to beguile you from the grief of a loss so overwhelming." He did however, in keeping with the season declare, "I cannot refrain from tendering you the consolation that may be found in the thanks of the republic they died to save."

On the very day Lincoln was assassinated he wrote a letter to General Van Alen, probably the last formal correspondence he composed, which was very appropriately a voluntary letter of appreciation and thanks. The concluding sentence follows:

"I thank you for the assurance you give me that I shall be supported by conservative men like yourself, in the efforts I may make to restore the Union, so as to make it, to use your language, a union of hearts and hands as well as of states."

Lincoln's Thanksgiving Proclamation

The year that is drawing toward its close has been filled with the blessings of fruitful fields and healthful skies. To these bounties, which are so constantly enjoyed that we are prone to forget the source from which they come, others have been added which are of so extraordinary a nature that they cannot fail to penetrate and soften even the heart which is insensible to the ever-watchful providence of Almighty God.

In the midst of a civil war of unequaled magnitude and severity, which has sometimes seemed to foreign states to invite and to provoke their aggression, peace has been maintained, the laws have been respected and obeyed, and harmony has prevailed everywhere, except in the theater of military conflict, while that theater has been greatly contracted by the advancing armies and navies of the Union.

Needful diversions of wealth and of strength from the fields of peaceful industry to the national defense have not arrested the plow, the shuttle, or the ship; the ax has enlarged the borders of our settlements, and the mines, as well of iron and coal as of the precious metals, have yielded even more abundantly than heretofore. Population has steadily increased notwithstanding the waste that has been made in the camp, the siege, and the battlefield, and the country, rejoicing in the consciousness of augmented strength and vigor, is permitted to expect continuance of years with large increase of freedom.

No human counsel hath devised nor hath any mortal hand worked out these things. They are the gracious gifts of the Most High God, Who, while dealing with us in anger for our sins, hath nevertheless remembered mercy.

It has seemed to me fit and proper that they should be solemnly, reverently, and gratefully acknowledged, as with one heart and one voice, by the whole American people. I do therefore invite my fellow citizens in every part of the United States, and also those who are at sea and those who are sojourning in foreign lands, to set apart and observe the last Thursday of November next as a day of thanksgiving and praise to our beneficent Father who dwelleth in the heavens. And I recommend to them that while offering up the ascriptions justly due to Him for such singular deliverances and blessings they do also, with humble penitence for our national perverseness and disobedience, commend to His tender care all those who have become widows, orphans, mourners, or sufferers in the lamentable civil strife in which we are unavoidably engaged, and fervently implore the interposition of the Almighty hand to heal the wounds of the nation and to restore it, as soon as may be consistent with the divine purposes, to the full enjoyment of peace, harmony, tranquillity, and union.

City of Washington,
 October 3, 1863.

Abraham Lincoln

What Americans Are Thankful For Today

Even during the dark days of the Civil War, with the nation divided, President Lincoln found much to be thankful for.

On April 10, 1862, he called upon the citizens to render thanks to God for signal victories of the land and naval forces and to pray for divine guidance for "our national counsels" so that peace and harmony might be restored. Again on July 15, 1863, he set aside the following Aug. 6 as a day of national thanksgiving for additional victories and as a day of prayer to "subdue the anger ... and change the hearts of the insurgents."

Shortly thereafter, on Oct. 3, 1863, Lincoln turned his eyes away from the battlefront, surveyed the nation as a whole, and found much to be thankful for not concerned with the travail of war. And he issued the thanksgiving proclamation, reprinted above, re-establishing a national day of thanksgiving for our spiritual and material blessings. The custom has been observed by every President ever since.

Seventy-four years before to the day, George Washington had issued a similar proclamation. In 1815, President Madison issued a similar call for national thanksgiving for the return of peace after the War of 1812. But although many governors proclaimed Thanksgiving Day in ensuing years, not until 1863, under Lincoln, did it return as a national festival.

Lincoln's 1863 proclamation has a tone that might well apply to 1954. Today, as in 1863, "needful diversions of wealth and of strength from the fields of peaceful industry to the national defense have not arrested the plow, the shuttle, or the ship." The nation is growing in strength and vigor. President Eisenhower's 1954 proclamation read in part:

"We are grateful that our beloved country, settled by those forebears in their quest for religious freedom, remains free and strong, and that each of us can worship God in his own way, according to the dictates of his conscience.

"We are grateful for the innumerable daily manifestations of divine goodness in affairs both public and private, for equal opportunities for all to labor and to serve, and for the continuance of those homely joys and satisfactions which enrich our lives.

"With gratitude in our hearts for all our blessings, may we be ever mindful of the obligations inherent in our strength and may we rededicate ourselves to unselfish striving for the common betterment of mankind."

As a nation, the people of the country are most thankful for the return of peace. Peace, in every generation, is Providence's greatest gift. Americans, too, are thankful for freedom and prosperity. No one can appreciate this better than those among us who have lived under totalitarian regimes.

Individually, Americans are grateful for good health, for their families and children, for good jobs. These observations may sound hackneyed, but they are still true as the Gallup poll on Page 52 shows.

People in every generation and in every country and clime would list these blessings as most deserving of thanks to the Almighty. And, as President Eisenhower says, we should unselfishly strive to make them enjoyed by all of mankind. When all the peoples of the world have cause for thanksgiving as much as our people, then, in Lincoln's words, there will be "full enjoyment of peace, harmony, tranquillity and union."

Cheers!

IT is no use trying to persuade some people to be happy. Worry and fear live with them like heckling in-laws, and even on Thanksgiving Day they enjoy not the cause but ponder darkly the effect—with an eye cocked to the package of bicarbonate.

But most of us, even with a sky filled with communist infernal machines, still are capable of enjoying the old-fashioned pleasure of this old-fashioned day.

It remains for the individual to decide what he should be thankful for on this day, of course. But after all, how dark is it? Abraham Lincoln, in the dark year 1863, still could give thanks for "the blessings of fruitful fields and healthful skies," and for the fact we had escaped war with England. More simply, Walt Whitman was grateful for "the midday sun, the impalpable air—for life, mere life."

To be sure, there should be a moment on Thanksgiving Day when we give sober thought to the hungry child keeping its rendezvous with death in India, or to the shell of a man in a communist torture cell. It is not shameful, however, but rather fitting, that we should fill the day with rejoicing for our own good fortune. "Go your way and eat the fat and drink the sweet," said the Lord to the Jews when they kept the "Feast of Weeks," and those were hard and fearful days, too.

So let us enjoy this day with easy conscience. For worry and fear there is always tomorrow.

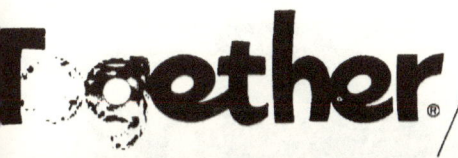

Together®

ARE CHURCHES SELF-CENTERED?
A Midmonth Powwow

METHODIST FAMILY-OF-THE-YEAR
Five Pages of Pictures

Midmonth Magazine for Methodist Families November 1962

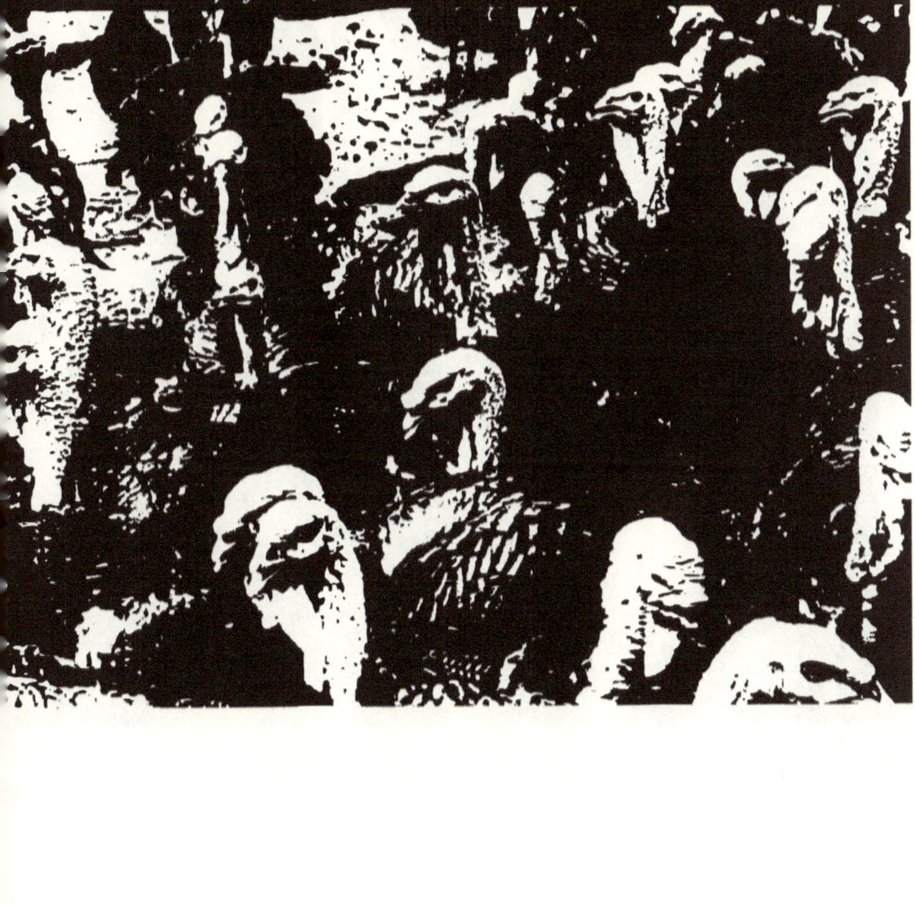

A Thanksgiving Proclamation

"*I do, therefore, invite my fellow-citizens...to set apart and observe t*
of thanksgiving and praise to our beneficent Father who dwelle

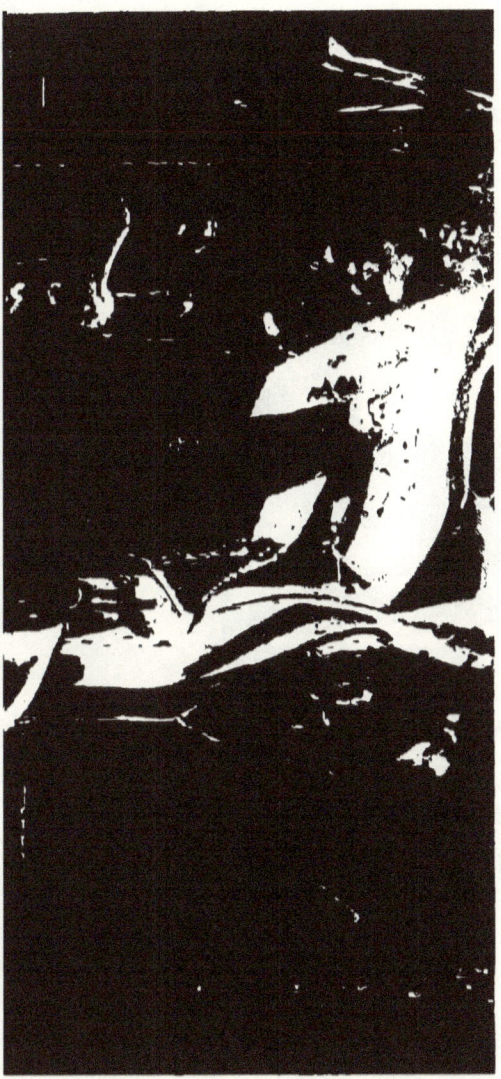

IT WAS October 3, 1863; the war between the North and South raged on, and Abraham Lincoln was weary with his anguishing responsibilities. Yet he could write:

"The year that is drawing toward its close has been filled with the blessings of fruitful fields and healthful skies. To these bounties, which are so constantly enjoyed that we are prone to forget the source from which they come, others have been added..."

With this introduction, acknowledging "the ever-watchful providence of almighty God," Lincoln crystallized as a national custom observance of the fourth Thursday of that November as a day of thanksgiving; and Dean Cornwell's splendid painting at left catches him after he has signed the wartime proclamation.

Americans had observed occasional days of thanksgiving and festival ever since 1621, when Gov. William Bradford declared the first one for the Pilgrims at Plymouth. And in years that followed, the custom spread to other colonies. At the end of the Revolutionary War, George Washington proclaimed Thursday, November 26, 1789, as a day for the new nation to thank God.

It is notable that in 1794, The Methodist Episcopal Church, then just 10 years old, recommended to all Methodists "that the last Thursday in October be set apart as a day of solemn and general Thanksgiving, and that all servile labour be laid aside, and those days be observed with all the solemnity of a Sabbath."

last Thursday of November next as a day

in the heavens." A Lincoln

Together

*takes great pleasure in announcing
that a Christmas gift subscription
has been entered in your name by*

Mr. and Mrs. John Doe)

*You will receive your first issue next
month. This portfolio is provided for
your convenience in keeping your issues
of TOGETHER intact. If you are
already a TOGETHER subscriber,
your subscription will be extended.*

gift subscription to TOGETHER

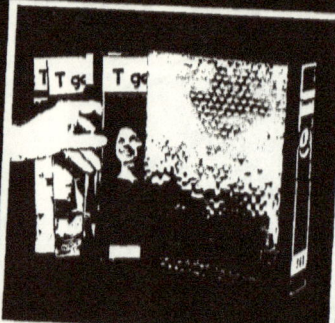

s. We'll send
every person
riptions and
for yourself.
ng so early.
r name will
Christmas.
nstructions.

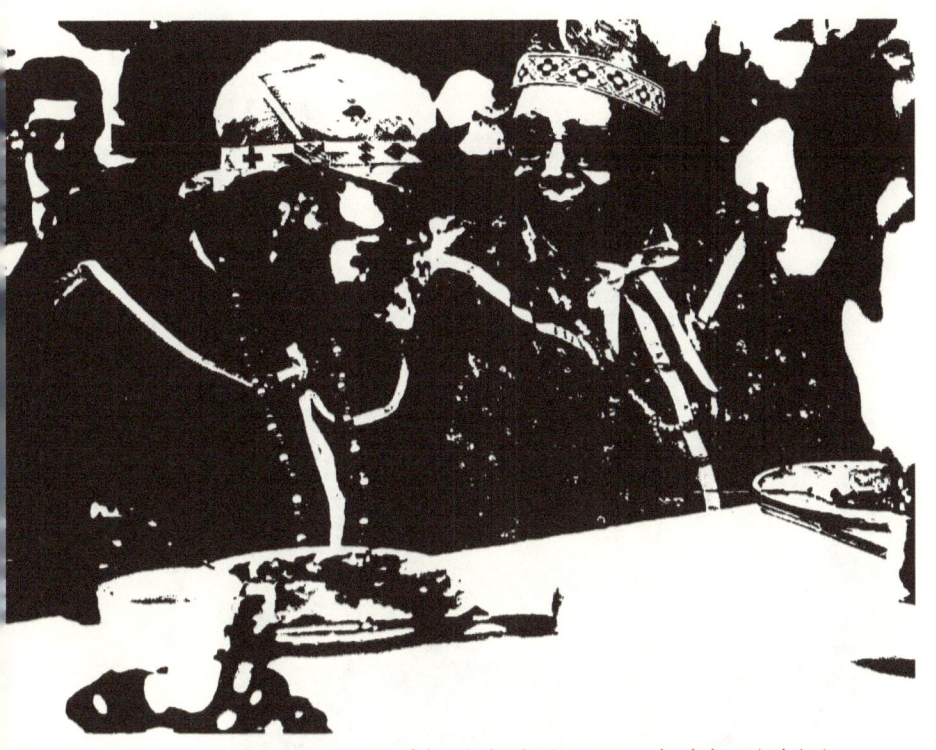

It is easy to imagine these two as grandmotherly matriarchs in the Five Nations of long ago. Centuries before woman suffrage, Seneca women played an important part in Iroquois life, even nominating members of the tribal council and removing them from "office" for misbehavior.

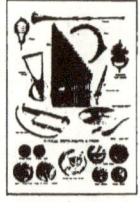
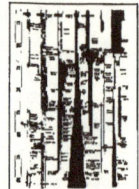

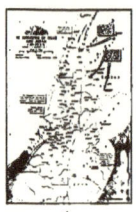

Lincoln's Thanksgiving Proclamation

The year that is drawing toward its close has been filled with the blessings of fruitful fields and healthful skies. To these bounties, which are so constantly enjoyed that we are prone to forget the source from which they come, others have been added, which are of so extraordinary a nature that they cannot fail to penetrate and soften the heart which is habitually insensible to the ever-watchful providence of almighty God.

In the midst of a civil war of unequalled magnitude and severity, which has sometimes seemed to foreign states to invite and provoke their aggressions, peace has been preserved with all nations, order has been maintained, the laws have been respected and obeyed, and harmony has prevailed everywhere, except in the theater of military conflict; while that theater has been greatly contracted by the advancing armies and navies of the Union.

Needful diversions of wealth and of strength from the fields of peaceful industry to the national defense have not arrested the plow, the shuttle, or the ship; the ax has enlarged the borders of our settlements, and the mines, as well of iron and coal as of the precious metals, have yielded even more abundantly than heretofore. Population has steadily increased, notwithstanding the waste that has been made in the camp, the siege, and the battlefield; and the country, rejoicing in the consciousness of augmented strength and vigor, is permitted to expect continuance of years with large increase of freedom.

No human counsel hath devised, nor hath any mortal hand worked out these great things. They are the gracious gifts of the Most High God, who, while dealing with us in anger for our sins, hath nevertheless remembered mercy.

It has seemed to me fit and proper that they should be solemnly, reverently, and gratefully acknowledged as with one heart and one voice by the whole American people. I do, therefore, invite my fellow-citizens in every part of the United States, and also those who are at sea and those who are sojourning in foreign lands, to set apart and observe the last Thursday of November next as a day of thanksgiving and praise to our beneficent Father who dwelleth in the heavens. And I recommend to them that, while offering up the ascriptions justly due to him for singular deliverances and blessings, they do also, with humble penitence for our national perverseness and disobedience, commend to his tender care all those who have become widows, orphans, mourners, or sufferers in the lamentable civil strife in which we are unavoidably engaged, and fervently implore the interposition of the almighty hand to heal the wounds of the nation, and to restore it, as soon as may be consistent with the Divine purposes, to the full enjoyment of peace, harmony tranquility, and union.

In testimony whereof, I have hereunto set my hand, and caused the seal of the United States to be affixed.

Done at the city of Washington, this third day of October, in the year of our Lord one thousand eight hundred and sixty-three, and of the independence of the United States the eighty-eighth.

A. Lincoln

THANKSGIVING DAY PROCLAMATION 1967

The first American tradition grew out of gratitude for survival.

It began -- long before independence was a dream -- with families responding to an even deeper human impulse. They had suffered the rigors of winter in a new world -- and they had endured. They put aside their plows and thanked God for the harvest's bounty.

Over the years, we have made Thanksgiving a unique national occasion. Thanking God for His goodness, we thank Him as well for the promise and the achievement of America.

Our reasons for gratitude are almost without number. We are grateful for the endurance of our government for one hundred and eighty years. We are grateful that the founding fathers planned so wisely for the generations that followed them. We are grateful for a material abundance beyond any mankind has ever known. In our land, the harvests have been good.

Much as we are grateful for these material and spiritual blessings, we are conscious, in this year, of special sorrows and disappointments. We are engaged in a painful conflict in Asia, which was not of our choosing, and in which we are involved in fidelity to a sacred promise to help a nation which has been the victim of aggression. We are proud of the spirit of our men who are risking their lives on Asian soil. We pray that their sacrifice will be redeemed in an honorable peace and the restoration of a land long torn by war.

We are grateful for the tremendous advances which have been made in our generation in social justice and in equality of opportunity, regardless of racial background. But we are saddened by the civil strife which has occurred in our great cities.

Recognizing the trials we have endured and are enduring, I have turned to the Thanksgiving Proclamation of President Abraham Lincoln in 1863. President Lincoln faced, with equal emphasis, both the blessings and the sorrows of the people.

He recommended to his fellow citizens that, "while offering up the ascriptions justly due to Him for such singular deliverances and blessings, they do also, with humble penitence for our national perverseness and disobedience, commend to His tender care all those who have become widows, orphans, mourners, or sufferers in the lamentable civil strife in which we are unavoidably engaged."

In a similar spirit I ask my fellow citizens to join their thankfulness with penitence and humility. Let us implore Almighty God that, to all our other blessings, He may add the blessings of wisdom and perseverance that will lead us to both peace and justice, in the family of nations and in our beloved homeland.

Americanism Holds Torch for World

By Sydney Harris

MOST PEOPLE FAIL to understand the difference between "patriotism" and "nationalism."

Patriotism is wanting what is best for your country. Nationalism is thinking your country is best, no matter what it does.

Patriotism means asking your country to conform to the highest laws of man's nature, to the eternal standards of justice and equality. Nationalism means supporting your country even when it violates these eternal standards.

Patriotism means going underground if you have to — as the anti-Nazis in Germany did — and working for the overthrow of your government when it becomes evil and inhuman and incapable of reform.

Nationalism means "going along" with a Hitler or a Stalin or any other tyrant who waves the flag, mouths obscene devotion to the Fatherland, and meanwhile tramples the rights of people.

* * *

PATRIOTISM IS A FORM of faith. Nationalism is a form of superstition, of fanaticism, of idolatry.

Patriotism would like every country to become like ours, in its best aspects. Nationalism despises other countries as incapable of becoming like ours.

Just as we fail to understand the difference between patriotism and nationalism so many people fail to understand what "Americanism" really consists of.

"Americanism" was something utterly new to the world when it was conceived by our Founding Fathers. It was not just another form of nationalism — indeed, it was a repudiation of all the then existing nationalisms.

It was conceived as a form of government unrestricted to one geographical place or one kind of people. It was open to all men everywhere — no matter where they were born or came from. In this respect, it was utterly unique. Its patriotism was potentially world-wide.

The word "Americanism" must not be narrowed or flattened or coarsened to apply only to one flag, one people, one government. In its highest, original sense, it asks that all men become patriots to an idea, not to a particular country or government. And this idea is self-government by all men, who are regarded as equals in the law.

This is why American patriotism—properly understood—is the best patriotism in the world, because it is for all the world, and not just for us. To confuse it with nationalism, to use it for ugly purposes, is to betray the dream of those who made it come true.

Thanks to all. For the great Republic—
for the principle it lives by, and keeps alive—
for man's vast future—thanks to all!

A. Lincoln

Thankfulness begets desire to give

CAL THOMAS

Today's expressions of thankfulness seem to be prepackaged and plastic—like "Thank you, Paine Webber," or "Thank you for shopping at K-mart and have a nice day," or "Thank you for using AT&T."

Perhaps our lack of genuine thankfulness has something to do with the fact that we have lost an object to whom or to which to give thanks.

The official Thanksgiving proclamations issued by the White House have long been written by an anonymous staffer who attaches the President's signature with the help of a machine.

In 1863 Abraham Lincoln not only wrote his own, he did not wait until Thanksgiving to issue a proclamation that called on the American people to be grateful for what they had, even in the midst of a civil war.

In April of that year, Lincoln indicted our great-grandparents in a way that perhaps no leader had before or since.

His purpose was to bring forth a spirit of repentance and confession for what he called our "presumptuousness."

Said Lincoln, " ... may we not justly fear that the awful calamity of civil war [and here you can insert our contemporary "calamities" of economic disorder, abortion, AIDS, family breakups and political uncertainties], which now desolates the land, may be but a punishment inflicted upon us for our presumptuous sins, to the needful end of our national reformation as a whole People?

"We have been the recipients of the choicest bounties of Heaven. We have been preserved these many years in peace and prosperity. We have grown in numbers, wealth and power as no other nation has ever grown. But we have forgotten God. We have forgotten the gracious hand which preserved us in peace and multiplied and enriched and strengthened us; and we have vainly imagined, in the deceitfulness of our hearts, that all these blessings were produced by some superior wisdom of our own. Intoxicated with unbroken success, we have become too self-sufficient to feel the necessity of redeeming grace, too proud to pray to the God that made us!

"It behooves us, then, to humble ourselves before the offended Power, to confess our national sins, and to pray for clemency and forgiveness."

This attitude of repentance, of gratitude, of thankfulness cannot be imposed from above. It must rise from below. A President can only show the way. He cannot force any of us down the road.

In my own experience I have seen the benefits not only of gratitude to God, but of thankfulness to parents, children, superiors and associates. It produces the results we mistakenly think we will get when we pursue goals with a spirit of selfishness.

The amazing truth about thankfulness is that it generates a greater desire to give on the part of both the giver and receiver. The one giving the thanks is appreciated and the one receiving thanks for his gift is encouraged to give again.

At Thanksgivings past we sometimes asked those at our table to say what they are thankful for. This year, in the midst of our current calamities, I will ask them to say who they are thankful for and why.

The person must be sitting at the table and everyone must give thanks to as well as receive thanks from a different person so that no one is excluded.

THAT SPIRIT CAN DO much for a family. As for a nation, Abe Lincoln had the right formula: "It behooves us, then, to humble ourselves before the offended Power; to confess our national sins, and to pray for clemency and forgiveness."

Daily News 11/26/87

DOES THIS LOOK FAMILIAR?

THANKSGIVING DAY IS FIXED ON THE LAST THURSDAY OF NOVEMBER

34. LINCOLN

Partly printed Document Signed in full as President, 4to, Washington, 20 October 1864.

Authorization for the Secretary of State to affix the Seal of the United States to "my Proclamation," of that date, being the setting aside by Presidential edict of the last Thursday of November as "a day of Thanksgiving and Praise to Almighty God..."

Thus Thanksgiving Day was first formalized nationally, although it had been celebrated, especially in the north, for a number of years, and there had been sporadic previous Presidential proclamations.

Some mounting residue on the fourth page, otherwise fine. Of course its appearance is the same as the similar seal affixing authorization, for the Emancipation Proclamation, sold at auction earlier this year for $192,500. But our document can stand on its own as a reminder of the wonderful American holiday, Thanksgiving. 15,000.00

THANKSGIVING: A CELEBRATION OF FAMILY, FAITH, AND NATION

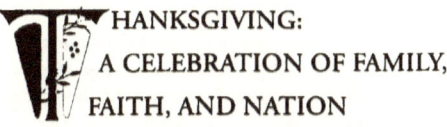

A holiday exhibit presented by The Lincoln Museum
Lincoln National Corporation, Fort Wayne, Indiana
November 29 to December 31, 1991

Since 1621, when the Plymouth Colony Puritans celebrated the gathering of their first harvest, Americans have
observed thanksgiving festivals and days of fasting and
prayer, particularly in times of war or other public danger. During the Revolutionary War military commanders
and political leaders appealed to the strong Protestant tradition of liberty and piety to help sustain Patriot unity
and morale. Continental Army chaplains not only enlist-
ed "God's superintending Providence" on the Patriot side,
but gave their sermons a decidedly republican cast.

Each year, between 1777 and 1784, the Continental
Congress set aside a day of solemn prayer and thanksgiving for God's blessings — foremost, the favorable
"interposition of Divine Providence" in the conflict with
Great Britain — and admonished the American people to
"the penitent confession of their manifold sins." As the
first President of the new United States, in 1789, George
Washington proclaimèd "a day of public thanksgiving
and prayer" to be observed on Thursday, November the
26th. After the wartime administration of President
James Madison (1809-1813), the responsibility for
officially proclaiming a day of thanksgiving fell to the
state governors.

The establishment of an annual Thanksgiving Day on "a national and fixed" basis was largely the work of Sarah Josepha Hale, the editor of the popular *Godey's Lady's Book*. As early as 1827, she urged a nation-wide observance of Thanksgiving Day; like the 4th of July celebration, it would be "an exponent of our Republican institutions." From 1848 on, she sent thousands of personal letters, in addition to her editorials, to state governors and other influential people, urging them to join in establishing the last Thursday in November as a national holiday. In the church calendar the last Thursday in November is the last day of feasting before the fasting and penance of the Advent season.

In her editorial of February 1860, hoping that the break-up of the Union could be averted, Mrs. Hale portrayed Thanksgiving as "the great Union Festival": "Let Thanksgiving, our American Holiday, give us American

President Abraham Lincoln signing the Thanksgiving Proclamation of 1863, by celebrated illustrator Dean Cornwell. Commissioned by the Lincoln National Life Foundation, the painting was first exhibited in 1938 on the 75th anniversary of the signing.

books — song, story, and sermon — written expressly to awaken in American hearts the love of home and country, of thankfulness to God and peace between brethren." Two and a half years of civil strife, with a staggering loss of life on both the Union and the Confederate sides, further strengthened Mrs. Hale's resolve. On September 28, 1863, still reflecting on the momentous Union victories at Gettysburg and Vicksburg, she wrote to President Lincoln and Secretary of State William H. Seward proposing that the President issue a proclamation setting aside the last Thursday in November, which fell on the 26th in 1863 (as it had in 1789), and "commending union Thanksgiving to each state executive."

Although it is probable that Secretary Seward actually wrote the Thanksgiving Proclamation of October 3, 1863, he was able to capture the compassionate and reflective mood that is apparent in the President's earlier Proclamations, especially his Proclamation of "national thanksgiving, praise, and prayer" of July the 15th, less than two weeks after the Battle of Gettysburg. The October 3rd Proclamation called upon the American people "as with one heart and voice" to "solemnly, reverently, and gratefully" acknowledge the "deliverances and blessings" of their angry, yet merciful, God, "with humble penitence for our national perverseness and disobedience." On October 20, 1864, acting perhaps on another reminder sent to Secretary Seward by Mrs. Hale, President Lincoln for the last time asked his fellow-citizens to observe the last Thursday in November "as a day of thanksgiving and praise to Almighty God, and recommended that they "offer up penitent and fervent prayers."

One of the most poignant and tragic ironies of the Civil War is that Southern, as well as Northern, nationalism took root in the soil of Puritanism and the heritage of the American Revolution. Confederate clerical, political, and military leaders claimed "God's special Providence for their cause and embraced the Puritan tradition of fast days, with sermons and public proclamations of humiliation, prayer, and thanksgiving. After the War, Southerners portrayed themselves as a Chosen People with a God-given mission to spread evangelical Christianity. Although the dream of a separate political nation in the South died in 1865, the dream of a separate cultural identity lived on with renewed vigor — finding expression in the "the religion of the Lost Cause."

⁂

SCOTT'S CONSUMER AFFAIRS

Thanksgiving

Kathy Honea, R.D.
Scott's Consumer Affairs Director

Although we may take Thanksgiving for granted, the day was not proclaimed a national holiday until the year 1863. Much earlier, of course, the Pilgrim Governor Bradford had sent some of his men out to shoot "wild fowl" so all the colonists might have a special manner to rejoice together. In 1789, George Washington proclaimed the first official Thanksgiving Day. However, the day was not declared a national holiday, and the custom did not endure throughout the entire country.

For twenty years, Mrs. Sarah Josepha Hale, editor of the widely read nineteenth-century *Godey's Lady's Book*, wrote letters to the current President of the United States and each Congressman, urging the proclamation of a national Thanksgiving Day.

In 1863, in the midst of a divisive civil war, President Lincoln heeded her pleas to "invite my fellow citizens in every part of the United States, and also those who are at sea or

who are sojourning in foreign lands, to set apart and observe the last Thursday of November next as a day of Thanksgiving and praise to our Beneficent Father."

Although the date has changed, the observance of Thanksgiving Day has continued throughout the years. In Lincoln's day, as now, Thanksgiving meant stuffed, roasted turkey with cranberry sauce, a variety of vegetables and relishes with pumpkin pie as the grand finale.

"PRESIDENTIAL" PUMPKIN PIE

This recipe is said to be a variation of old fashioned pie that was a favorite in the White House for generations.

10	Eggs, separated	1 tsp.	Mace
4 c.	Pumpkin	1 Tbsp.	Cinnamon
2 c.	Dark Brown Sugar	2 Tbsp.	Brandy
½ tsp.	Nutmeg	6 c.	Whole Milk
		2	Pie Shells, unbaked

Beat separately the 10 eggs whites and 10 egg yolks. Add the yolks to the cooked, strained (or canned) pumpkin.

Add brown sugar, nutmeg, mace, cinnamon; mix well. Add brandy.

Fold the stiffly beaten egg whites into the mixture and beat with electric mixer.

Slowly beat the whole milk into the mixture. Pour into 2 unbaked pie shells.

Bake 20 minutes in 425°F. oven; then reduce heat to 325°F. for 30 minutes.

YIELD: 2 Pies

ll Scott's Are Open 24 Hours Every Day

ORT WAYNE, INDIANA ANGOLA, IN COLUMBIA CITY, IN

The Miracle Harvest

By Arthur Quinn

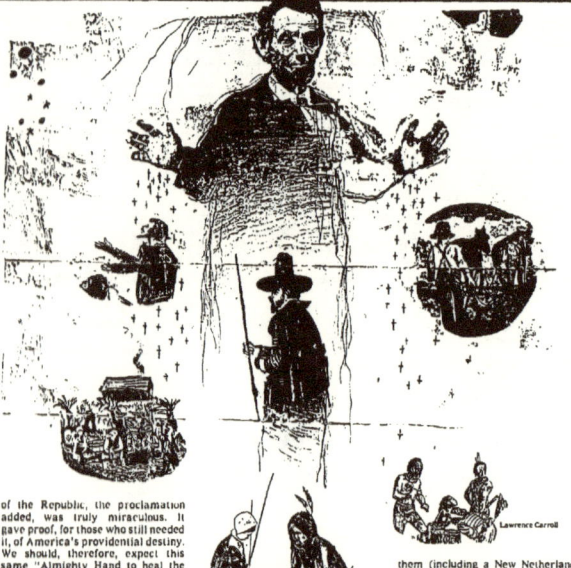

Lawrence Carroll

BERKELEY, Calif.
The last time I was in Plymouth, I found myself eavesdropping on a tour group. These modern pilgrims were, not surprisingly, disappointed by the famous rock. Looming like a Gibraltar in our national mythology, Plymouth Rock was in fact a sad little boulder under a Victorian awning. Then a question was asked about Thanksgiving, the Pilgrims' other claim to fame: "What kind of a farmer has a harvest festival in late November?" Answer: "A bad one."

I had to bite my tongue. The first Thanksgiving dinner was actually held in October — October 1621. Plenty early for a harvest festival. Perhaps I should have told the tourists that the November date was Lincoln's doing, in 1863. But that might have required a disquieting explanation, for what we often forget is that we as a nation get Thanksgiving not from the Pilgrims but from the Civil War.

The Thanksgiving tradition was still alive and well in the Northeast (with locally fluctuating dates) when Abraham Lincoln became President. But it had not caught on nationally. In declaring Thanksgiving a national holiday, Lincoln gave it so late a date he detached it from its agricultural origins. This was fitting, since he intended to use the holiday for political purposes.

In that autumn of 1863, the Civil War had taken a bad turn for the North. After the victory at Gettysburg in July, Maj. Gen. George G. Meade had allowed Robert E. Lee's army to slip away, to live to fight another day. The Union was then defeated at Chickamauga — and the Union command was left, in Lincoln's words, "confused and stunned like a duck hit on the head." The country, Lincoln knew, was itself becoming increasingly confused and stunned by the sheer magnitude of the carnage. The casualties at Chickamauga alone were being estimated at more than 35,000.

So Lincoln was, quite understandably, worried about the coming election, particularly about the American people's continued willingness to gather in this vast harvest of death. The Thanksgiving proclamation can thus be read as a first salvo in his re-election campaign. This proclamation did concede that the Civil War was "of unequaled magnitude and severity." But it asked the nation to view the losses from a broader vantage:

"Needful diversions of wealth and of strength from the fields of peaceful industry to the national defense have not arrested the plow or the shuttle, or the ship; the ax has enlarged the borders of our settlements, and the mines, as well as of iron and coal as of the precious metals, have yielded even more abundantly than heretofore."

This continued prosperous growth

Arthur Quinn's most recent books are "A New World," a history of colonial America, and "The Rivals," a narrative of the California Gold Rush and the coming of the Civil War.

of the Republic, the proclamation added, was truly miraculous. It gave proof, for those who still needed it, of America's providential destiny. We should, therefore, expect this same "Almighty Hand to heal the wounds of the nation" and to restore peace and tranquility and union "as soon as may be consistent with Divine Purposes."

One Lincoln admirer caught the religious spirit of the proclamation when he exclaimed in response, "No ruler of millions, since King David the Psalmist, has clothed great thoughts in sublimer language."

Well, perhaps. But I cannot help wondering about the original Pilgrims. What would they have thought of Lincoln's use of their modest harvest feast?

They would not have objected to a Thanksgiving feast in the face of horrific death. Their own feast had been just that. They had arrived in Plymouth in the winter, a group of about 100, inadequately supplied and weakened by the anxious months of preparation and the arduous voyage.

The Pilgrims, Lincoln and fields of bones.

As a result, during the ordeal of that first winter, approximately half the colonists died, including the governor. Women routinely sacrificed themselves for their families — whether the mothers gave up their own food or just worked themselves into exhaustion in caring for the sick, 13 of the 18 wives died, but only 3 of the 20 children.

Moreover, the Pilgrims had survived their ordeal, if barely, only because a previous people had not. The colonists had found Plymouth deserted but with many signs of previous inhabitants. They found large corn caches, without which they almost certainly would have starved. They also found human bones scattered around — not just the occasional skeleton but piles of them, as if this had

been a battlefield where corpses had been left to rot. The Pilgrims subsequently learned that the Pawtuxet Indians who lived there had recently been wiped out by an epidemic, a catastrophe that would become all too familiar to the indigenous peoples of eastern North America.

Squanto, the lone Pawtuxet who survived because he had been kidnapped by European sailors before the epidemic, adopted this strange new people occupying his ancestral lands. And at their first Thanksgiving dinner in 1621, the Pilgrims acknowledged that they had a harvest to celebrate largely because of the advice of their new friend. As for the numerous dead innocents, the Pilgrims did not need to remind themselves that the works of Providence were usually inscrutable to human reason.

Nonetheless, a true Pilgrim would have been appalled at Lincoln's proclamation — not because of its general thanks amid innocent suffering but because of its politically cunning appeal to religion.

The Pilgrims were separatists, Protestants who had despaired of a true reformation of European society. Even to be part of such a corrupt society was to risk being polluted or entirely swallowed up. The only alternative was to seek a hallowed seclusion, to separate from the greedy, struggling, self-seeking world, to live in an artificial circle of exclusion from ordinary humanity.

They had first fled to the Netherlands. They were not persecuted there, but they did struggle incessantly against the insidious erosion of their community by Dutch prosperity and cosmopolitanism. So they heroically set out for the New World, and for a time they seemed to thrive in their own peculiar way. But then, as colonies became established around

them (including a New Netherlands on the Hudson), the erosion began again, and this time their leaders had no heroic remedy to offer. Plymouth would eventually be absorbed into the far more ambitious and aggressive Massachusetts Bay Colony.

The Pilgrims' greatest governor, William Bradford, would look back on the early days of Plymouth with a perplexed sadness as he brooded over their failure. But he never lost his conviction that God speaks only through pilgrim peoples, separate and small and weak. As for the eventual appropriation of Thanksgiving by a great and prosperous nation, this was exactly the pollution of godly religion by worldly politics that he and his people had fled Europe to escape. But in the final analysis they failed. The world eventually despoils everything within it.

Nevertheless, we, if any reverence for the distant Pilgrims and their beliefs be in us, should at least remember on this day that our Thanksgiving, like our America, is not theirs. The holiday of Thanksgiving is properly of Lincoln and of our bloody crucible as a people, the Civil War. □

FEMININE WRATH. — In the fall of 1863, after the great national successes at Vicksburg, Chattanooga, and Gettysburg, the President of the United States appointed a day of Thanksgiving to God for the victories that had crowned the national arms.

The Bulletin, a Union paper published in Memphis, Tennessee, made a simple announcement of the fact, and remarked that there were many, no doubt, in that city who would heartily join in celebrating the day. This suggestion drew upon the editor's head the following glowing and defiant

philippic from the pen of one of the fair citizens of Memphis:

"EDITOR BULLETIN: You call attention to Lincoln's appointment of a day of Thanksgiving for the successes which have blessed our cause, and you hope the day will be properly observed. By 'our cause' you mean the Union cause. I wonder how you think the people of Memphis can thank God for the successes of the Union Abolition cause. You pretend to think that a great Union sentiment has sprung up in Memphis, because you say that upwards of eleven thousand persons have taken the oath of allegiance. Let me tell you, if they have taken it, they did not do it of their own free will, and they don't feel bound by it; they had to take it under a military despotism, and don't feel bound to regard any oath forced upon them in that way. Do you believe that any preacher in Memphis will appoint services in his church at Lincoln's dictation? Let one dare to try it, and see how his congregation will stand it. They know better. They know full well that the people of Memphis give thanks over Union disasters with sincere hearts, but don't rejoice at Union victories, as they call them. The women of Memphis will stick to the Confederate cause, like Ruth clung to her mother-in-law, and say to it, 'Where thou goest I will go, where thou livest I will live, where thou diest I will die, and there will I be buried.' But where are your great successes? Your own papers say that Lee brought off a train of captured spoils twelve miles long, and that Morgan destroyed seven or eight millions of dollars' worth, before all Ohio and Indiana could stop him. Pretty dear success, this. Still I won't rejoice over it at Lincoln's dictation. But wait till President Davis' day comes round. Perhaps by that time Meade may get another whipping, and if you don't see rejoicing and thanksgiving then, you may well believe that you and your officious local fail to see half that exists in Memphis. Now you won't publish this, perhaps, because it don't suit you. You can say the reason is, because I don't put my real name to it. You can do as you please about it. I choose to sign it.
                        MARY LEE THORNE.

Thanksgiving

Again we come together all
  To keep in the good old way,
Just as they did in days of yore,
  A glad Thanksgiving day.

Call to Thanksgiving

Washington appointed Thursday, November 26, in 1789, as a day of thanksgiving, but it was Lincoln who established the precedent which is now followed. Lincoln appointed the fourth Thursday of November, 1864, and since that time each President has annually followed his example.

BY JOHN H. CUTLER

It is generally believed that Thanksgiving Day as we know it today began after the first harvest in the fall of 1621 when the Pilgrim Fathers at Plymouth set aside a period for fasting and offering thanks. That was when Governor Bradford sent four hunters out with their fowling pieces to bag a plentiful supply of game.

They came back with enough turkeys, which were than abundant in Massachusetts, to feed the entire community. The Pilgrims celebrated for "almost a solid week of public and private entertainment," the records say. All very true, but it was President Abraham Lincoln, and not Governor Bradford, who began our national Thanksgiving Day as we now know it.

In 1863 Lincoln designated Thursday, Aug. 6, as a definite day of thanksgiving, but later in the same year he returned to the precedent set by Washington and set aside the "last Thursday of November next as a day of thanksgiving."

George Washington, in the first thanksgiving proclamation issued by a President of the United States, in 1789 designated Thursday, Nov. 26, as the holiday. He chose the last Thursday of November, and it was that day that was later adopted as a precedent.

A Legacy

The early records show that there were all kinds of days of thanksgiving originally. As an annual festival, it is clear that our present celebration is a legacy from the Forefathers, but only by a long chain of circumstances. Long before the colonists left England it had been the custom to observe special thanksgiving days after events of national significance. When Sir Francis Drake whipped the daylights out of the Spanish armada in 1588 two separate days were set apart by the English church as special days for offering thanks.

The Puritans had no special day of thanksgiving at first. It was their practice to offer thanks after a good harvest, the arrival of a ship, or their deliverance from or victory over an enemy. At first they chose Wednesday or Thursday for their combined religious and festive celebrations, in order to have them as far removed as possible from the Sabbath, which they observed austerely. Thus after the first harvest in 1621 they set aside just one more period for relaxing and offering thanks.

To that feast, as every schoolboy knows, they invited Massasoit, who brought along 90 of his tribe and remained at the festivities for three days. The Pilgrim Fathers in New Plymouth, like the Puritans, had festivals after each harvest, it is believed. In 1622, referring to the abundant harvest, Governor Bradford wrote: "For which mercie (in time conveniente) they also sett aparte a day of thanksgiving."

Solemn Observance

In 1623 there was another such day, and Bradford referred to a "day of thanksgiving to our merciful God" in 1631. Meanwhile, among the Puritans of Massachusetts Bay, thanksgiving days were from the outset observed more solemnly. For instance, on Feb. 22, 1630, a day of "friend-bringing and food-bearing ships," and on Nov. 4, 1631, after the harvest, Governor Winthrop had this to say: "We keep thanksgiving day today in Boston."

The day fell at various times. June 19, 1633, was one 'for the Puritans, the reason not being known. In 1639 Connecticut observed a similar holiday, and in 1644 the Dutch of New Netherland followed suit. It is true, however, that from the beginning there was a tendency for thanksgiving days to become annual events in Massachusetts, as well as in Connecticut. But for no particular reason.

When word came to Boston on July 3, 1745, that British and colonial troops had captured Louisburg, the following Thursday was named a City for public thanksgiving. During the Revolution the Continental Congress set aside one such day at least once a year, but the event was not scheduled very far in advance. It depended on how the war progressed.

Not until 1789, then, did Congress by joint resolution, urge the Chief Executive "to recommend to the people of the United States a day of public thanksgiving and prayer, to be observed by acknowledging with graceful hearts the many and signal favors of Almighty God, especially by affording them an opportunity peaceably to establish a form of government for their safety and happiness."

Further Confusion

In 1789 the Episcopal Church appointed the first Thursday in November as the holiday. There was further confusion in 1795 when Washington named Thursday, Feb. 19, as the day. The reason was the suppression of the Whiskey Insurrection.

Three years later President John Adams added to the variety by selecting Wednesday, May 9. His thanksgiving didn't even fall on a Thursday. Things then proceeded quietly until President James Madison chose the third Thursday in August of 1812. Later he observed the holiday on the second Thursday in April in 1815 to commemorate the cessation of hostilities with England.

Some 49 years later President Lincoln resumed the custom by issuing proclamation dated April 10, 1862. He "recommended to the people of the United States that at their next weekly assemblages in their accustomed places of public worship, which shall occur after notice of this proclamation shall have been received, they especially acknowledge blessings, etc . . ." Lincoln did not appoint any special day.

Southern Objections

Why did no Chief Executive set aside a day of thanksgiving for 40 years? The reason was the objections raised by the Southern States. They considered such holidays legacies of "Puritan bigotry," and argued that no President should issue proclamations in their behalf. Hence, any celebrations of this nature that did exist during those decades existed in the North.

Lincoln finally decided on the last Thursday probably because Washington had done so, and it had proved to be the most popular day for thanksgiving. But long before Franklin Delano Roosevelt did a little shuffling, President Andrew "first Thursday of December" as the holiday. In 1866 he returned to Lincoln's date, and the last Thursday has since been the traditional day.

Thanksgiving Day, in capital letters, is today observed in all the States of America, and it is a legal holiday in all but a few of them. The custom has spread to Canada since 1872, but since 1921 their day of thanksgiving has been the Monday of the week containing Armistice Day, or Nov. 11. It's all very confusing, what?

Our present holiday is a bit different from the one the Pilgrims celebrated in 1621. The turkeys and pumpkins cost more, and the festivities last one day instead of close to a week.

Thanksgiving Day Not Started by Pilgrim's Governor Bradford But by President Lincoln

Lincoln Reprieved Turkey

One year, a few weeks before Thanksgiving, a friend sent a fine live turkey to the White House, with the request that it be served for President Lincoln's dinner. Tad, the President's son, who was the life of the White House, took a great fancy to the bird, naming it Jack and feeding and petting it. He even taught it to follow him about.

Just before Thanksgiving, while the President was discussing important business with a cabinet officer Tad rushed into the room, sobbing with anger. The turkey was about to be killed! And Tad had flown to the President to lay the case before him and save Jack.

"But," said the President, "Jack was sent here to be killed and eaten."

"I can't help it," blubbered Tad between sobs. "He is a good turkey and I don't want him killed!"

The President of the United States listened gravely, and then taking a card wrote an order of reprieve. Tad seized the card and rushed away. The turkey's life was saved.—Our Dumb Animals.